"What are the chances that the police will have the hacked computer?" Luke asked.

"Very low, and–" Dani paused to meet his gaze to ensure he was listening "–even if we do find it, I have no proof that you didn't use this laptop then discard it yourself."

He fisted his hands. "Then what do you need to clear my name?"

Good question. "At this point, I don't see anything that will clear your name short of finding the real hacker."

His shoulders slumped in defeat. He peered at Dani, and the agony in his eyes made her draw in a breath at his vulnerability. She should probably heed the evidence or lack of evidence, but despite nothing pointing to his innocence, she didn't think he was guilty.

Or was she just hoping that the man who sparked something inside her that she'd thought long dead was innocent of a terrible crime like treason?

Books by Susan Sleeman

Love Inspired Suspense

High-Stakes Inheritance
Behind the Badge
The Christmas Witness
*Double Exposure
*Dead Wrong
*No Way Out
*Thread of Suspicion

*The Justice Agency

SUSAN SLEEMAN

grew up in a small Wisconsin town where she spent her summers reading Nancy Drew and developing a love of mystery and suspense books. Today she channels this enthusiasm into hosting the popular internet website TheSuspenseZone.com and writing romantic-suspense and mystery novels.

Much to her husband's chagrin, Susan loves to look at everyday situations and turn them into murder-and-mayhem scenarios for future novels. If you've met Susan, she has probably figured out a plausible way to kill you and get away with it.

Susan currently lives in Oregon, but has had the pleasure of living in nine states. Her husband is a church music director and they have two beautiful daughters, a very special son-in-law and an adorable grandson. To learn more about Susan, please visit www.SusanSleeman.com.

THREAD OF SUSPICION

SUSAN SLEEMAN

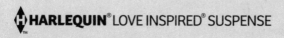

HARLEQUIN® LOVE INSPIRED® SUSPENSE

Recycling programs
for this product may
not exist in your area.

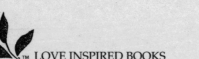 LOVE INSPIRED BOOKS

ISBN-13: 978-0-373-44557-8

THREAD OF SUSPICION

Copyright © 2013 by Susan Sleeman

All rights reserved. Except for use in any review, the reproduction or utilization of this work in whole or in part in any form by any electronic, mechanical or other means, now known or hereafter invented, including xerography, photocopying and recording, or in any information storage or retrieval system, is forbidden without the written permission of the editorial office, Love Inspired Books, 233 Broadway, New York, NY 10279 U.S.A.

This is a work of fiction. Names, characters, places and incidents are either the product of the author's imagination or are used fictitiously, and any resemblance to actual persons, living or dead, business establishments, events or locales is entirely coincidental.

This edition published by arrangement with Love Inspired Books.

® and TM are trademarks of Love Inspired Books, used under license. Trademarks indicated with ® are registered in the United States Patent and Trademark Office, the Canadian Trade Marks Office and in other countries.

www.Harlequin.com

Printed in U.S.A.

To every thing there is a season and a time
for every purpose under the heavens.
—*Ecclesiastes* 3:1

To the brave men and women of the military.
Thank you for your heroic service to our country.

Acknowledgments

Thanks to:

My family—my husband, Mark,
who doesn't cringe when I ask for help.
My daughter Emma for helping me plot and edit
this book, and Erin for your continued support.

Elizabeth Mazer—your insight and editing
take my writing to the next level.

Ron Norris—retired police officer with the
LaVerne Police Department. You provide me with
police, weapon and military details on a timely basis.
Any errors in or liberties taken with the technical
details Ron so patiently provides are all my doing.

And most important, thank You, God, for
reminding me that Your timing is always perfect.

ONE

Luke Baldwin's training as a Navy SEAL warned him he was in trouble. To pay attention, be still and take precautions. But darkness clawed at his senses, keeping him from fully waking and heeding the warning.

Hoping to get his bearings, he concentrated on the sounds unfolding around him. Cars whizzed by. Horns honked. If he were home in bed where he should be, he'd hear the quiet of suburban life, not Portland's bustling traffic.

Digging deeper, he managed to pry his eyes open and look around. He sat behind the wheel of his battered Jeep Wrangler tipped at an angle in the ditch with the hood pressed against an enormous Oregon pine. Thick underbrush had swallowed up his car and spindly pines swayed overhead in icy winds.

"What in the world?" He shook his head to clear his mind. Razor-sharp pain stabbed between his eyes. He let the lids fall, hoping to end the blinding intensity. Nausea curled his stomach and burned up his throat as the damp cold of winter seeped to his bones.

How had he ended up in the ditch?

C'mon, Baldwin, think.

He breathed deeply, letting oxygen rush to his brain and stem the nausea. Clarity tugged the edges of his mind, then suddenly it all came flooding back.

He'd been driving home in the wee hours of the morning

to grab a quick shower before today's demonstration of his company's software. The roads were slick with rain, and fog hovered over the pavement. Driving too fast for the conditions, he'd felt his car start to slide. He'd pumped the brakes. The pedal had sunk to the floor with no resistance. His car had left the pavement, slipping into the ditch and ramming the tree. With no airbags, his head had slammed into the wheel and everything had gone black.

His ancient Jeep had failed him again. Of course it had. It was on its last legs and needed replacing. He should get a better car. One with reliable brakes and airbags. Not happening, though. He'd poured all of his money into his company.

Wait. Company. What time is it?

He glanced at his watch: 1030 hours.

No! Couldn't be. He'd be late for the demonstration.

He released his belt and dug out his cell phone. Dead.

"No, no, no!" He pounded the wheel, the lancing pain slicing up his arm and into his already throbbing head.

Just what he deserved for failing his staff. His software company vied for a multimillion-dollar military contract today at 1100 hours. He could kiss the money and his company goodbye if he didn't show up.

Not an option for a SEAL, even a former one.

He forced open his door, the bent metal groaning and creaking. He stumbled out. Rain spit from the gray winter skies, dampening his mood even more. He grabbed fistfuls of grass and pulled his aching body up to the winding road leading into Portland. He waved at cars, hoping to flag one down, but they sped past as if he were invisible. He'd have to hoof it down the hill to the coffee shop where he got his caffeine fix every morning. They knew him and would let him use their phone.

He hunched into his jacket to fight the wind whistling down the hill and jogged down the road. Ignoring the pain pulsing through his body, he settled into the zone he'd often found as a SEAL after silently dropping behind enemy lines. His mind floated free, and oddly, his father's voice rang in his head.

So you screwed up again. I knew you'd never amount to anything.

Maybe his father was right. He was a screwup. He'd failed most everyone who mattered in his thirty-four years on this earth. His mother, his older sister—both of them killed in a fire set by his crazed father. His fiancée, Wendy, who'd wanted more from him and had every right to expect it before she'd bailed two years ago. And Hawk. Poor Hawk.

Luke flashed back to Afghanistan, to before he'd left the SEALs to be close to his only living sister, Natalie. Insurgents had rushed his SEAL team—guns blazing in the night, his buddy Hawk falling and never getting up again. All courtesy of an intercepted satellite phone call. Luke had held Hawk as he took his dying breath and made a promise to prevent other soldiers' deaths because of satphone security issues. So he'd founded SatCom with Hawk's little brother, Timothy Revello, and their dream was moments from becoming a reality.

If Luke made it to the office before he broke that promise.

He upped his speed and soon swung into the coffee shop, heat instantly cocooning him as the scent of aromatic java perked him up. The owner stood behind the long mahogany bar, a line of customers waiting for their drinks. With no time to wait in line, Luke approached Earl.

Earl placed a cup in front of a young woman, then looked up. "Man, Baldwin. You look rough."

Luke's chest burned from exertion, but he managed to say, "Need your phone, Earl. Car and cell dead. Need to call a cab."

Earl grabbed a cordless phone and a laminated cardstock listing local phone numbers, then slapped them on the counter with a solid whack. "Want your usual when the line gets down?"

Luke nodded, and as he worked to bring his breathing under control he requested a cab, then dialed his partner, Tim's, direct line at SatCom.

He tapped his foot on the floor as he waited, and caught sight of his scruffy appearance in the front window. A lump, swollen and purple, stuck out on his forehead. A cut on his cheek gaped open and blood saturated his wrinkled pants and shirt. No wonder people were staring at him. He might need to go home and change before the demonstration. *If* Tim thought he could handle it. A big *if* for the introverted geek who'd rather walk on a bed of nails than speak in public.

"Revello," Tim finally answered, sounding out of breath.

"It's Luke."

"Where are you?" Tim demanded. "I've been going crazy here."

"I'm sorry." Luke took a quick moment to regroup and not let Tim's frantic tone up his own anxiety. "I ran my car off the road on my way home last night and knocked myself out. I called a cab and should be there in forty minutes tops."

"Forty minutes?" Tim shouted. "You better hope we're still in business by then."

So much for changing clothes.

"Can you stall with General Wilder? Just until I get in."

"Probably, but Wilder's not our biggest problem right now."

"What's going on?" Luke asked calmly, though his heart had kicked into high gear again.

"The procurement committee got an anonymous call late yesterday afternoon claiming our software has been sabotaged."

"What?" Luke barked out.

"Yeah," Tim said. "Wilder sent over a consultant to validate the program. She was waiting at the door when I got here. She's been evaluating the software and our network logs all morning."

"This is a joke, right? To get back at me for being out-of-pocket and making you worry."

"Nah, man, it's no joke."

"So let me get this straight," Luke said, dread settling over him. "We're minutes from demonstrating our software for the military brass and they send an independent consultant to validate it? Just because some crackpot calls and says it's corrupt?"

"Not just any consultant, but Dani Justice." A waver of uncertainty threaded through Tim's voice.

"You make it sound like she's well-known in the computer world."

"Tops in our field."

"And we're sure the general contracted with her?"

"Yep. Confirmed it with his aide before I let her in the building." Tim paused and a long sigh filtered through the phone.

This can't be happening. "You know anything about this Dani Justice?"

"Yeah, she's legendary in the Portland computer world. She once worked for the FBI in cyber crimes. Now she and her siblings own a private investigation company." Tim snorted. "Working in a mom-and-pop agency seems like a waste of all that talent, but what do I know."

"I should've known Wilder would hire the best."

Earl called out Luke's coffee order, his face creased with his usual easygoing smile.

Luke held up a finger and smiled back despite his inner turmoil. "Too bad Wilder didn't give us a heads-up."

"He said they couldn't warn us she was coming or we might try to cover up the software's vulnerability."

"We'd never do that. *If* there was a vulnerability, that is." Luke craned his neck, hoping to see his cab pulling up.

"I know, but Wilder thinks someone at SatCom is guilty.

The aide said if they find even a hint of sabotage, Wilder would pursue prosecuting the guilty party for treason."

"Treason!" Luke shouted, the entire coffee shop stilling. He lowered his voice. "That's a pretty serious charge for tampering with software."

"I know, right, but we both know if someone sabotaged it, they could listen in on the military's satellite phone conversations."

"And lives would be lost," Luke added. His gut clamped down as he imagined how the information gained by altering their software could give the enemy an upper hand. Field operations would be vulnerable. Locations known. Soldiers under fire. A shudder claimed Luke's body.

He had to get to the office. Where was his cab? "Before I go, please assure me that Ms. Justice won't find anything wrong with our software."

"We should be good. We've done our due diligence and hired people to validate it. We got a clean bill of health."

Unease niggled at Luke's gut. "But we didn't hire Ms. Justice like the general, did we?"

"Are you kidding? We could never have afforded her."

"If you'd come to me I would've found the money somewhere, Tim. You know that."

"Where? You're completely tapped out. You've already sold your house and moved in with your sister. You've even maxed out your credit cards and company loans. So where would this cash come from?"

"Still—"

"I know, I know," Tim interrupted. "If you've told me once you've told me a thousand times. You'd rather our company fails than deploy anything that could put service personnel in danger."

"It's not just talk, you know. I mean every word of it."

"Believe me, I got it." Tim sighed as he usually did when

they talked about commitment to honor and sacrifice that soldiers lived and breathed, but Tim had no clue about.

If a SatCom employee had actually tampered with the software and planned to put soldiers at risk, Tim wouldn't believe they deserved to be charged with treason, but Luke did. Even if the lost contract forced SatCom into bankruptcy or if, as the owner of the company, his name and reputation would be tainted for life.

If they don't bring you up on charges, too, and you don't end up in a prison cell of your own.

Espionage, Dani Justice thought as she stared at her monitor in the minuscule SatCom office.

Someone had remotely hacked into SatCom's network last week and left a gaping hole in the software. After the military deployed this software to their satphones, the hacker could access their calls and sell information to the highest bidder. And that was unacceptable.

Question was, who would do such a thing? Was it one of the owners, Timothy Revello or the conspicuously absent Luke Baldwin? She was hired to locate the problem, not prove who perpetrated it, but she couldn't let a traitor go free.

She could track the transmission through the internet service provider, and that meant she needed Derrick's help. She dug out her phone and dialed her twin brother.

"Do you still have that friend at Northwest Internet?" she asked the minute he answered.

"Yeah," he replied skeptically.

"I need an address for one of their clients."

He didn't respond right away, and she was tempted to ask again. But while she made snap decisions, he often needed to process information first, so she waited, tapping her foot on the floor and feeling as if time physically ticked away. She glanced at the clock on her computer. The demonstration would start any minute now, and she needed to get to the conference room to tell General Wilder and his joint military committee about her findings.

"I don't know, sis," Derrick finally said. "Stan's a contact you don't want to burn. He's helped me a lot lately, and I don't want him to get into trouble."

"This is important, Derrick."

He snorted. "You always say that."

"This time I mean it." He'd agree if she offered details of her discovery, but she wouldn't do that until she'd put together a comprehensive report for their family's private investigations agency.

"You promise you won't ask me to talk to Stan again after this?"

"Promise," she said, but her response didn't ring true even in her own ears.

"That didn't sound real convincing."

"It's hard to make a promise like that. What if we faced a life-or-death situation and Stan could save someone's life? I'd go back on the promise then. Or what if—"

"Enough." He laughed good-naturedly. "I got it. I'll call Stan."

She rattled off the network login information Stan would need. "This is urgent. As in, I need the information now."

"Don't worry. I got it. I'll get back to you as soon as I can." He disconnected.

She went back to the software and started her written report for the general. In less than ten minutes, her phone chimed a text. She grabbed it from the desk and smiled when she saw Derrick had come through with the address she needed. She plugged it into a database they often used to locate people, and a name flashed on the screen in front of her.

"Really?" she whispered in surprise as she spotted the name of a SatCom associate, then sat back with a satisfied sigh.

God was smiling on her today. She'd located her first ever

traitor, possessed the evidence to prove it and was only moments away from exposing him at the demonstration.

Inside SatCom's modern two-story building, Luke rounded the corner to the conference room. The three-member military procurement committee and two of his staff members sat around a long table. Tim, wearing his usual jeans and a long-sleeve T-shirt, paced at the head of the table. A tall, slender woman with softly waving blond hair stood at the side. Her back was to Luke, but he could still see her hands in motion as she spoke.

The infamous consultant Dani Justice, he assumed. And if she was attending the demonstration, their software was most likely corrupt as the anonymous caller had claimed.

Could this be the end of his company? Of his reputation? Of everything he'd worked for?

He dragged in a breath but came up thirsting for more, his heart racing.

Breathe, he told himself. *Just slow down and breathe. Your team needs you. Fight the problem, but do it the right way.*

Calm. Respectful. Befitting a former SEAL.

He slowed to compose himself. No point in barging in the room with a crazed glare as if he'd crawled out of a combat zone.

"Your software has been altered, Mr. Revello." Ms. Justice's voice, filled with passion, carried out the door. "I found a backdoor, fully compromising it."

Luke's feet completely faltered for a moment as shock from her confirmation washed over him. A surprised murmur traveled through the committee and several mouths dropped open. Luke had no clue what a backdoor was, but he clearly understood someone had compromised Crypton as the anonymous caller had claimed.

"Is this possible, Mr. Revello?" General Wilder asked, though his expression said he'd already decided it was true.

He thinks we sabotaged the software on purpose. Luke's heart sank.

"No one here would do such a thing," Tim answered emphatically.

Ms. Justice pulled her shoulders back, looking even taller than the five-ten or so he pegged her at. "The software wasn't modified internally. It was done by remotely logging on to your network."

"No," Tim said again, but this time his voice had fallen to a whisper. "Our network security is top-notch."

Tim was melting down. Luke needed to get in there. He rushed toward the door.

"Do you have proof of this breach, Dani, and can you find the person responsible?" Wilder asked.

She took a few steps closer to the table. "The best I can do until I have time to dig deeper is to give you the physical address where the transmission originated."

Luke stepped into the room and met Wilder's quizzical gaze. He came to his feet, his chair shooting back and hitting the wall as whispers filled the room. "Baldwin," he said. "You look terrible. Are you all right?"

"I'm fine." Luke smiled, but he had to force his lips to turn up. "I apologize for being late. I ran off the road last night and was trapped in my car until an hour ago."

Wilder let wizened eyes rove over Luke. "And you're sure you're fit to be here?"

"Fine."

"Then you should know there's a problem." Wilder took his seat. "We were just about to start the demonstration when Dani told us the software has been sabotaged."

"I heard her outrageous claim from the hallway." Luke met Ms. Justice's damning gaze, firing back with as much strength as he could muster.

She crossed her arms. "It's not outrageous, Mr. Baldwin. I have verifiable proof that your network was remotely accessed and the software modified." The zeal in her large brown eyes told Luke she spoke the truth.

"I will, of course, need to see the proof, but at least we now know about the issue and can fix it." Luke faced Wilder again. "Since the sabotage came from outside the company, I hope you'll give us a chance to correct the problem and still consider Crypton for this contract."

"I'm sorry if I wasn't clear, Mr. Baldwin," Ms. Justice jumped in, her full focus pinned on Luke. "The transmission may have come from outside the company, but it originated from a SatCom employee's home address."

"What?" Wilder slammed a hand on the table making everyone jump. "Give us the address, Dani, so we can expose this traitor."

She rattled off a local address, her eyes never leaving Luke's face.

Impossible.

Shock iced over Luke's heart and his legs felt as if they would no longer hold him upright. He hissed out a breath and searched for a response that not only wouldn't end his career, his company, his dream, but also wouldn't land him in jail for espionage.

Ms. Justice took a deep breath then added, "I'll let Mr. Baldwin tell you who resides at that address."

Luke couldn't speak.

"You obviously know who lives there," Wilder said after a few moments, his focus locked on Luke. "I suggest you share it with us, or the committee and I will walk."

Luke planted his hands on the table for support, pulled back his aching shoulders and met Wilder's penetrating gaze head on. "I live there, General. It's my home address."

TWO

Unbelievable. Dani stared at Luke Baldwin as she sat at the end of the table.

He hadn't reacted as expected. No denial of the charges. No explanation. He'd simply come to his full height and snapped his shoulders into a hard line as if he were standing at attention before his commanding officer. Now he stood ramrod-stiff, looking all soldier. All Mr. Tough Guy. Still, she'd seen his face pale and those broad shoulders slump for a moment after her announcement.

His employees huddled in the corner, frantically whispering. If Luke noticed, his expression didn't give it away. Not surprising. As a former SEAL, he'd developed the ability to hide his emotions.

He suddenly swiveled, his gaze searching the room like a heat-seeking missile looking for a target. His cobalt eyes locked on hers, and she drew in a sharp breath at the intensity. He advanced toward her with the stealth of a large cat, radiating power and demanding attention—hers and everyone else's in the room.

She was powerless to look anywhere but at him. She took in the three-inch gash, swollen and raw, running over a high cheekbone, and a purple goose egg stretching the tanned skin on his forehead. Underneath his injuries, he was ruggedly handsome, and she caught herself staring as her heart rate sped up. At the other end of the table, Wilder paused, his finger in midair as if making a point to the stunned committee members gathered near him. His eyes tracked Luke, and the committee members followed suit.

But Luke passed them by and didn't stop until he reached her, his nearness even more unsettling. He peered down on her from his over-six-foot height, his expression earnest. "No matter what you discovered in Crypton, I didn't sabotage it. I'm not a programmer. Far from it. My computer skills end at knowing how to email and surf the internet."

"Please, Mr. Baldwin. You expect me to believe you have no computer skills and yet you started a software company."

"Call me Luke." He squatted down, his presence filling the space in front of her. "My expertise is the military way of life and how our product is used in the field. Tim handles all of the programming."

She fired a skeptical look at him, and he quickly held up his hands. "I get that it sounds crazy, but I lost a good friend in Afghanistan due to compromise of our satellite phones. Before Hawk died, I promised I'd find a way to solve the problem and make sure no one else lost their life from the same issue. So I sought out his brother, Tim, and we formed the company."

Sounded reasonable. Honorable, even. Exactly what she'd expect from a former SEAL. But could she believe him? He hadn't faked his brief response to her announcement, of that she was sure. But he'd recovered quickly. Too quickly, settling a mask of indifference over his face. Did he not know about the sabotage, or was he upset that he'd been caught? She hadn't a clue which to believe.

"Look," he said, his voice low as if he didn't want the others to overhear. "I don't even know what a backdoor is." Looking fatigued, he dropped a knee to the floor, bringing him even closer and giving her a good look at the exhaustion etched in his eyes. "In fact it'd be helpful if you'd explain it to me. In layman's terms, please."

Was this claim of a lack of computer skills his attempt to cover up his involvement in the sabotage? She appraised him. His eyes were clear and guileless. She'd give him the benefit of the doubt. For now.

"A backdoor is exactly what it sounds like," she said. "Think of it like a door to a house or building. Sometimes we enter from a back door so we don't draw attention to ourselves. A backdoor in software is the same. It lets the person who modified the software slip in undetected to modify the program."

Luke sucked in a short breath. "It's true, then. Our sworn enemies could hear satphone conversations and know the military's every move."

Dani could tell he was thinking about the loss of his friend, but she couldn't sugarcoat the potential damage just to make him feel better. "He'd have to hack through military defenses once the software was deployed, but after reviewing the backdoor code, I can tell you the saboteur is very skilled and it wouldn't be hard for him to do so."

"That rules me out, then." He clenched his jaw and corded muscles in his neck stood out. "Besides, what motive could I possibly have to sabotage my own software?"

"If you hadn't gotten caught, you could've sold any secrets you overheard to the highest bidder."

He jerked back as if she'd slapped him. "I'd never do that, but I get that you have to suspect me."

She didn't want to doubt him, but what choice did she have?

"I'd like to hire you to dig deeper into this mess and prove my innocence," he continued. "But the only way I'll be able to pay you is if I can somehow convince the general to give us another chance and the contract goes through." He paused and looked at the general and his committee. "Given their unsympathetic expressions, I'd say it's highly improbable, but I hope you'll agree to help anyway."

Interesting. "Money aside, what if things don't go your way and I prove you're guilty? You know I won't ignore it. I'll have to turn you in."

"I'm certain that won't happen." He offered her a flicker of a smile.

She had to fight not to return it with one of her own. She was so intrigued by him—by the case—that she wanted to jump up and shout, "Yes, I'll help you!" But she knew nothing about this man other than he was a SEAL. She'd like to think that meant he was trustworthy, but SEALs were just men with razor-sharp skills. Fallible. Susceptible to greed and criminal actions like any man.

The big question was, could she help someone suspected of treason? She wanted to. His case would be the perfect chance to use her computer degree and the skills she'd learned working cyber crimes at the FBI. Skills that had been underutilized since she'd joined her family at the Justice Agency.

Right, the family. They'd have to agree. She'd fulfilled her obligation to the general, so that wouldn't be a problem. But getting her family on board was another story.

"I'd have to run it by the agency first," she said, wondering if her siblings would even consider working with a suspected traitor.

"Agency?" he asked.

"I haven't properly introduced myself." She held out her hand. "Dani Justice of the Justice Agency. It's a full-service agency owned by my family. We handle all private-investigation needs, including computer crimes."

"Ah, you must be the family spokesperson. Or at the very least the one in charge of commercials." He took her hand in his and smiled. Not the forced number he'd used a moment ago, but an irresistibly devastating grin. He captivated her in a way no man had in a long time, and the heat from his touch traveled up her arm. His smile suddenly fell and he let go of her hand.

Embarrassed at her reaction, she tucked her hand behind her back. "All joking aside, I can talk to my siblings about adding you to our client list."

He narrowed those startling blue eyes. "What are the odds that they'd agree to take me on?"

"Honestly," she replied as she sought the answer, "not good. My brother Cole is a former National Guard member and won't agree at all." She paused and thought about the emotional turmoil from fighting a war that Cole had only recently healed from. "And after everything he went through during two tours in Iraq, I'm thinking the group will support him and say no to you."

A flash of disappointment claimed his eyes before he cleared it away. "I guess I'll have to find someone else, then."

The same disappointment settled inside her heart, and she wished she could do something. She'd waited for the perfect case to prove her abilities since joining her siblings. Even at thirty-two, as the youngest female of five adopted siblings, she was often babied and never allowed to take charge on a case. She was desperate to do so.

There had to be a way to do it. There just had to.

He started to rise.

"Wait." Impulse had her shooting out a hand to stop him. "I'll do it."

He arched a brow. "Not that I'm not thankful, but are you sure?"

"Positive. If you're truly innocent, then someone else either used your computer or hacked your home network. I might be able to prove it by looking at your home computer. That could cast enough doubt on your guilt, and I can bring my family on board."

He nodded. Once. Quickly. Decisively. Then he glanced at

Wilder and his group. "I'll need time to talk with the general and my staff, and then we can head to my place."

"Great," she said.

He slowly came to his feet, agony lighting on his face. His eyes darkened into a shade of steel that burned a path ahead, and he walked away. She imagined him in his uniform in Afghanistan, facing down terrorism. He'd be a formidable foe.

She watched him march up to Wilder, and uncertainty plagued her heart.

Had she done the right thing in agreeing to help him? Or would she soon find herself dealing with a cunning traitor who expertly knew how to use his charms to get his way?

Luke pushed from his desk and strode to the conference room. His adrenaline from the car crash and shock over the sabotage had disappeared hours ago, fatigue taking its place. As he approached the long table where Dani awaited him, he swayed and felt as if he might drop to the floor. He grabbed the edge of the tabletop for support, but when he caught Dani watching him, he let go and came to full height.

Never let anyone see your weakness, his father had warned so many times that, even though Luke had lost respect for his father long before he'd died, he often found himself living by the man's misguided code.

Making sure his shoulders were back in military precision, he crossed the room and forced out a smile for Dani. "I've had a rental car delivered, and I'm ready to head to my house. I'll meet you there, since you already know my address."

She opened her mouth but didn't seem to know how to respond.

"Sorry. The comment about you knowing my address was my attempt at a lame joke to lighten the mood."

She smiled, and if he wasn't so exhausted, he might take the time to enjoy how it lit up her face and chased the confusion from her eyes.

He held out his hand. "After you."

She grabbed her laptop case and he slipped it from her hands. She stopped and looked him in the eye. "I appreciate the gesture, but I carry my own computer." She took the case from him and shouldered it before striding down the hall.

Stubborn, much?

He set off, but a wave of dizziness assailed him and he had to run his hand along the wall to keep up with the *clip, clip, clip* of her pointy heels. In the elevator she watched him carefully. He expected her to speak at any moment, but she said nothing. They stepped into the cooling afternoon air, and he dug his keys from his pocket.

With long fingers she snatched them out of his hand. "You're in no shape to drive."

"I'm fine," he said, though he clearly wasn't fine if a slight 115-pound female could best him and take his keys. He reached for them, but she slipped her arm behind her back.

The quick motion sent his head into a spin again, and he wobbled for a moment.

She considered him with an unwavering gaze. "You should see a doctor before we go to your house."

Not sure what to do with his hands when all he wanted to do was reach behind her and grab his keys, he shoved them into his pants pockets. "I've been through far worse than this, and I know when to seek medical attention."

She lifted her chin. "And I have three brothers who would all be as foolishly stubborn in this situation. So trust me. I have plenty of skills in dealing with it." She looked him dead in the eye. "I'll drive and we'll make a stop at the E.R. on the way. That is, if you still want me to take this case."

"Fine," he said, not liking it one bit, but knowing he needed to play by her rules if she was going help him. "Lead the way."

She pivoted sharply and set off. Not needing to hide his less-than-optimum performance any longer, he followed at his own pace. He should be royally miffed at her, but he respected her determination, and his anger quickly subsided. He liked a woman who knew her own mind. Even better when the mind was encased in a captivating package.

He met her at her SUV and climbed into the passenger seat next to her. The subtle scent of her coconut fragrance wrapped around him. Feminine and tough at the same time.

What man could resist such a combination?

She laid her arm along the top of his seat and backed out of the space. As she returned her focus to the front, their gazes met for the briefest of moments. He got lost in her eyes, and interest in a woman that had lain dormant for years flared to life. She quickly jerked her gaze away, but before she did, he saw the same spark of interest.

You've got a great sense of humor, God, sending this woman into my life after all these years and at the worst possible time.

Not really expecting God to talk back, given Luke's strained relationship with Him, Luke turned to look out the window. He caught Dani's reflection in the glass and that little zing sparked again.

He stifled a groan and reminded himself of all the reasons why getting involved with any woman right now was a bad thing. Working with Dani Justice was going to be interesting. Maybe too interesting for his own good.

The sun was setting in glorious oranges and reds behind the West Hills by the time Dani pulled into Luke's driveway and parked behind his rental car. After extensive testing, the E.R. doc had cleared him to drive, so they'd retrieved his car from SatCom and she'd followed him to his town house.

Long, uncomfortable silences had populated their time together, and she almost dreaded getting out of the car, but she had a job to do. She grabbed a flashlight, and as she walked toward the front door she searched through the light drizzle and thick fog blanketing the lushly landscaped property.

In one of their brief discussions, Luke had claimed to have sunk all his money into his company, and yet he lived in one of Portland's most exclusive areas. Dani's sister, Kat, had bought a foreclosure home in the area, so Dani knew the high price of property here. Luke could be renting, she supposed. Or maybe her initial instincts about him were totally wrong, and he wasn't who he seemed.

"Nice property," she said, trying not to sound obvious in her search for an explanation.

He watched her for a few moments, then grinned with that magnetic smile he seemed to flash freely. "For a P.I., you're not very good at fishing, are you?"

Her irritation instantly flared, but she wasn't sure if it was because he saw right through her or because her pulse kicked up whenever he grinned with boyish charm, in direct contrast to the imposing man standing before her. Either way, she wouldn't let him see her reaction.

She gave him an innocent smile. "I've never been much for fishing. I'm a city girl through and through."

"Too bad." His smile widened, one corner crookedly tipping higher. "I could've shown you all the best fishing holes in the area." He opened the door, then turned back. "Oh, and in answer to your unspoken question, the town house belongs to my sister, Natalie."

Ugh! She'd known him for only a few hours and yet he seemed to think he was always right. So confident. Everything she was attracted to in a man. Sure, he was good-looking—fit, muscular with a swagger that spoke to his self-assurance— and she'd have to be blind or near death not to react to him. But men like him were off-limits for her. He was too much like her ex-boyfriend, Paul. She'd found his confidence attractive, too. Until six months ago, when he'd gone all controlling and stalker on her. She wouldn't put herself through that ever again. Not for any man.

"You can go on in," she said, trying to sound unaffected

by anything he said or did. "I'd like to do a quick inspection out here."

His brow went up in question, and he held his position.

She'd have to explain if she wanted him to go inside. "I need to see if there are signs of a break-in. If your computer was used without your permission, they would've had to break in or access your wireless connection from close by."

"I hadn't thought about that."

"That's why I'm the private investigator and you're the client." She kept her voice free of the sarcasm that wanted to creep in. "I'll be just a minute."

He nodded but stopped mid-nod when a flash of pain darkened his face.

"You should take something for the pain," she suggested.

He straightened his spine. "I'm good."

Right. Mr. Tough Guy. "It's not a sign of weakness to accept help, you know."

"Come in when you're finished," he said, changing the subject. After a protracted look, he went inside and closed the door.

"Fine, be in pain, then," she mumbled as she often had when her stubborn brothers refused to listen.

She shone her flashlight over the property, checking the windows for pry marks. She continued around the home, catching a welcoming wave of light spilling from floor-to-ceiling windows in the backyard. As she glanced into the family room, she spotted Luke leaning against a counter in the adjoining kitchen, talking on the phone. Even if he hadn't just told her that the town house belonged to his sister, the feminine decor screamed he wasn't the owner. She was certain he wouldn't abide floral prints of any kind in his home, and she had to admit neither would she.

She finished circling the town house and stood in the driveway, making a quick sweep of the neighborhood. A security camera on the home across the street pointed down their driveway, which meant Luke's place would show up in their footage and it might prove useful.

Useful if she cleared Luke's name and if she found herself searching for another suspect, she reminded herself as she headed for his front door.

Since he was expecting her, she didn't knock but entered the two-story foyer with an open staircase. Through the rich mahogany banister she could see the family room and the adjoining kitchen island.

"Luke," she called out.

"In the kitchen," he responded.

She found him still resting against the counter, his phone to his ear. He held up a finger and told the person he was talking to that he had to go.

"That was my sister, Natalie." He stowed his phone. "I figured you'd want to look at her computer, too, so I got her permission."

Not something a man with a secret to hide would do. Was he really a ruthless traitor and he planned to set up his sister? Or could his sister be behind the sabotage?

"Did you find anything outside?" He pushed off the counter, coming closer.

She took a step back, garnering a quirk of his eyebrow. So what if he knew she was being cautious? He was a former SEAL. He could end her life in a moment if he so chose.

"There were no signs of forced entry, but the people across the street have a security camera pointed in the direction of your house. If I determine a break-in did occur, we may have the suspect on video."

"They're good friends with Nat, so I'm sure they'll share the video if we need it."

"Good to know," she said. "I'd like to look at your computers if you'll show me where to find them."

"This way." He led her toward the back of the house.

She crossed the gleaming wood floors and shook her head

as she imagined this big hunk of a guy trying to get comfortable on his sister's dainty sofa and chairs in the family room. He stepped through French doors into an office with an ornate desk sitting in the middle of the room and white bookshelves circling the perimeter.

"The laptop is Nat's. She lets me use her old desktop." He gestured at an older model computer, the monitor sitting by a pricey ultrathin laptop.

Dani's gaze flew to his face. "You don't own your own computer?"

"No."

She watched him carefully, looking for a hint of deception. "Kind of odd for a guy who owns a technology company not to have a computer."

He lifted a shoulder in the briefest of shrugs. "The world needs computers, but I'd rather my life was free from things I can't control."

So he was a control freak like her twin brother, Derrick. Not the only one in her family, but he was the worst when it came to her. Balking anytime she did anything the least bit risky and if he didn't get his way, losing his temper. As a result, she pushed harder. Even going into law enforcement when a career in information technology was her first dream.

She dropped onto the desk chair as Luke grabbed a straight-back chair. He turned it around and straddled the seat. "Will this take long?"

"Depends on what I find." She booted up the computer and the laptop.

As she worked, she could feel his eyes on her. She didn't look at him but watched the screen wake up, then called up the needed information. She ran through several screens but found she couldn't concentrate with his piercing eyes tracking her every move.

She looked at him. "This would be a lot easier if you didn't stare at me like that."

"Sorry," he said, looking sheepish. "It's just you're nothing like I expected for a computer guru."

"Is that so?" She appraised him.

"I expected someone like Tim and the rest of my programming staff. You know…kinda geeky. Wearing a T-shirt with an odd saying that only computer professionals understand. Shy, not real good with people. Not someone like you with your…your…well, you know." His face turned the color of a ripe tomato, so out of character for the charmer she'd seen so far.

She'd had this same discussion a hundred times with other people and knew he meant she was fashionably dressed and attractive. Not that she was conceited, but she'd been told enough times that God had blessed her with above-average looks. But the big, bad military man was too embarrassed to say it. Oddly this more than anything else he'd said or done since she'd met him made her believe in his innocence and made her want to put him at ease.

"Minus the T-shirts, I am that person," she offered. "I just don't look the part. I work hard to overcome the shyness, and trust me, if you saw my Star Wars collection, you'd know I'm a real geek at heart."

For a moment, he didn't seem to know how to take her response, but then he tipped back his head and laughed, an altogether pleasant sound.

When his laughter stilled, she said, "So can I get back to work without you watching my every move now?"

"I could stand to get cleaned up, I suppose." He stood and she saw the pain light in his eyes for a moment before he cleared it. This guy didn't want anyone to see he was weak, and yet it was his weakness that made him seem human to her.

As he left the room, she dug into his computer files. Thirty minutes later, she knew without a doubt that even an inexperienced hacker could have used his home network to access

Crypton on the night in question. But what she found next threw her a curveball.

"Interesting," she whispered as she wondered what her findings meant.

She heard footsteps heading her way, and she looked up to see Luke returning. She didn't want to stare at him, but how could she not? He wore pressed tactical pants in a dark brown, a light tan T-shirt that molded to his toned physique and his damp hair was even darker and brought out the penetrating blue of his eyes. He was the complete physical package, and she was more attracted to him than she'd first thought. Something that hadn't happened since Paul's reign of terror.

Why now, God? Why him?

"Have you found anything?" he asked, oblivious to the battle raging inside her.

She forced her mind back to the job. "Yes, but I don't know what to make of it yet."

"Can you explain it in simple terms that I can follow?"

She swiveled the monitor so he could see it, then tapped the screen. "These entries are from your and Natalie's computers. The entry shows you both used your wireless router to connect to the internet the day before SatCom was hacked. Notice the two IDs."

He nodded. "Since the IDs are different, does that mean each computer has a different ID?"

"Exactly, and that lets me see who accessed the internet the night in question." She opened another log. "This is the day SatCom was hacked. You can see one computer logged on to the internet, and the ID is different from the first two I showed you."

He leaned closer to look at the screen, his fresh minty scent filling the air. "I don't understand how that can be. We only have the two computers you see here."

"What about a visitor? Did you or Natalie have a friend over that night?"

"Not at three in the morning."

"Then the only thing that makes sense is that someone used your wireless network from outside your home. To do that your network would need to be unsecured."

"Nat takes care of all of that stuff," he said quickly— maybe too quickly in hopes of covering himself. "At least she did until her computer crashed a few days ago. She had to call in a friend to help her. He found a virus on her computer." He shook his head. "Another reason I don't like computers much. I prefer to be able to see my enemies."

"Did the friend access your network with his computer?"

"I don't know. Can't you tell by looking at the logs you've been reviewing?"

"I can tell a computer other than your laptop or your sister's desktop accessed your network, but without seeing the friend's computer, I can't tell if it was his."

"I can call Nat and ask him to bring it over."

"That would be great."

As he made the call, Dani tuned him out and pondered the puzzle before her. What motive might the friend have for sabotaging SatCom? For that matter, what motive might Luke's sister have?

Dani would need to run a background check on both of them and prove a connection to SatCom before considering them strong suspects. At this point, Luke still held top spot on her list.

Assuming his guilt, had he used another laptop to do his dirty work, then hidden or disposed of it? But then why log into SatCom from his home, where it could be traced?

Made no sense. The only other explanation was that the network wasn't secure on the day SatCom was accessed. That she could check easily enough.

She pulled up the wireless router log and scanned the data. The settings had been altered a few days ago, well after Sat-Com's hack. Maybe the friend who fixed Natalie's computer had changed the settings to block other viruses. If Dani had been called in to fix Natalie's computer issues, she would've secured the network, and she guessed the friend had done the same thing.

Luke's conversation was coming to a close, but Dani signaled to him not to hang up yet.

"Hold on, sis," he said, turning his attention to Dani.

"Will you ask Natalie if her friend altered the network security settings?"

Luke asked the question. A few moments later, he said, "She says he didn't connect to the network with his computer that night, and he said something about making things more secure, but Nat doesn't know exactly what he did."

"Thanks," Dani replied. "As long as he drops by with his computer tonight, that's all I need for now."

Luke said goodbye to his sister and stowed his phone.

She waited for him to look at her again. "When did this friend work on Natalie's computer?"

"I don't know. Do you need the exact date?"

"If you don't want to go to jail, I do."

He cringed and moved back.

"Look," she said. "I'm sorry for being so blunt, but since I've cleared your computers, we can assume no one broke in here to use them. And with the current security settings, the likelihood of access coming from outside your house is minuscule. But I found a change made to the settings, so I suspect the friend helping your sister modified the settings to protect her from another virus. If this happened *after* the login to SatCom, we can prove the network was accessible before that day."

He raised his head in thought. "I think it was last Tuesday. No wait…Monday. I remember because the Seahawks were playing, and her friend commented on the game."

She checked the dates again. "That correlates with the date I found."

"So this means someone could have accessed our network from outside the house before then, right?"

"Right."

The tension in his expression loosened. "Is there any way to find the computer that was used?"

"Maybe. The hacker might have used a stolen computer to cover his trail and ditched it afterward. I've seen something like this happen when I worked cyber crimes for the FBI."

"So if it *was* stolen, might the police have it in evidence?"

"Possibly, but the identifying information we need wouldn't be in their reports. We'd have to physically look at each computer." Her mind whirled over steps she could take to locate the computer. "My sister, Kat, is married to a Portland police detective. She should be able to get access to the computers they have in evidence."

"What are the odds that they'll have it?"

"Very low, and—" she paused to meet his gaze to ensure he was listening "—even if we do find it, I have no proof that you didn't use this laptop, then discard it yourself."

He fisted his hands. "Then what do you need to clear my name?"

Good question. "I'll have to find the real hacker to fully clear you. But you should know, if it's not your sister or her friend, finding the hacker will be as difficult as finding a needle in a haystack."

His shoulders slumped in defeat. He peered at Dani, and the agony in his eyes made her draw in a breath at his vulnerability. She should probably heed the evidence or lack of evidence, but despite nothing pointing to his innocence, she didn't think he was guilty.

Or was she just hoping that the man who sparked something inside her that she thought long dead was innocent of a terrible crime like treason?

THREE

Luke stared out his office window, the morning sun already high in the sky over SatCom's parking lot. A silver SUV like Dani's wound through the lot and pulled into a visitor's space. He held a hand over his eyes to block the sun and confirm the vehicle belonged to her. She climbed out, but even with the early-morning chill, she didn't wear a coat. She wrapped long, slender arms around her waist as she hurried toward the building.

Good. He'd hoped she'd arrive early so they could get to work on finding the real traitor. He eagerly made his way toward the small reception area to meet her. She'd taken a seat in a leather club chair and was looking at her phone. Her long legs were crossed and her foot swung in rapid arcs as if she were eager to get to work. She wore jeans again today, dark and pressed with a military precision that he could appreciate. Her shoes were more practical than yesterday's and her top a vivid red that highlighted her fair coloring.

She was such a study in contrasts. Tough and determined, yet fragile. On the one hand, he found her to be sensible and grounded. On the other, she did things like not wearing a coat when the weather called for it and supporting him when the facts screamed his guilt.

She looked up and caught him watching. Her eyes, the color of rich cappuccino, locked on his, and he was riveted until she looked away and jumped to her feet. She headed toward him, and he noted a hint of concern in her expression.

Luke braced himself. He didn't know if he could handle more bad news. "Is there something I need to know?"

"We need to talk." Her voice held a definite edge that he hadn't heard before. "In private." She didn't wait for him to respond but hurried toward the exit.

He had half a mind not to follow her, to keep from hearing another problem. But he wasn't one to run from his troubles, so he trailed her outside. She stopped on the sidewalk and a strong gust of wind hit hard. A shiver rippled over her body. He took off his jacket and tried to settle it over her shoulders, but she stepped back.

"I'm just trying to be a gentleman," he said, watching her carefully.

She gave him that same I-can-take-care-of-myself look she'd fired at him several times yesterday, so he shrugged back into his coat.

Strands of her long, silky hair whipped into her face, and she impatiently swatted it out of the way. "Mitch Elliot, my brother-in-law who's a cop, came through for us. Kat and Mitch spent a good part of the night personally reviewing every computer in evidence and found the one we're looking for."

"That's great," he said, wondering why she'd felt a need to be secretive about this. "How did the police get it?"

"They picked it up during the bust of a small-time burglar. We don't think he has anything to do with the network hack, but he might be able tell us where he got the computer. This is a perfect time of day to catch him at home, so I'm heading over to talk to him now. I thought you might want to come with me."

"Are you kidding? I wouldn't miss it."

"Then let's go, and I'll give you the details on the way." She held out a remote to click open the doors on her large

SUV, then flashed a mischievous smile at him. "After your accident yesterday, I'm thinking you don't have a very good record behind the wheel, so I'll drive again."

Despite her adorable smile, he wanted to argue but didn't want to admit he had a thing with letting other people drive. He climbed into the passenger seat and slid it back to accommodate his legs.

She slipped behind the wheel as gracefully as she did everything else. Not at all like he'd expect from a P.I. and definitely not from an FBI agent. He could easily see how criminals like the man they were going to talk to might subdue her.

Luke would have to keep a watchful eye on her—no hardship, that was for sure. But no matter how intrigued he was by her, that was as far as things would go. He had too many unsettled issues for that to ever be a possibility in his life.

She turned the key, and the powerful engine roared to life, then purred smoothly. "You seem like you're in less pain today."

"I am," he said and waited for her to demand additional details as she always seemed to do.

Surprisingly she concentrated on winding her way out of the lot. While she merged the car seamlessly into heavy morning traffic, Luke called Tim to tell him he'd left the building and to ask him to inform his assistant so she didn't worry. He'd already shared with Tim that they'd hoped a stolen computer was used to access the network, but despite questions Tim fired off, Luke kept the nature of this trip to himself. He didn't want Tim to lose hope if the lead didn't pan out.

"You really care about Tim, don't you?" Dani asked when he'd stowed his phone.

"You can tell that from a simple phone conversation?"

"You're reserved and cautious when you talk to people, but when you talk with Tim, your whole demeanor changes."

He shook his head. "I need to remember you think like a P.I., assessing everything I say and do."

"And I need to remember you're a former SEAL doing the same thing."

"Touché," he said and laughed.

"So back to Tim."

"I think I mentioned he's Hawk's little brother." Mindful of Dani's observations, Luke worked hard to keep the emotion over the loss of his friend from his voice. "I figure the least I can do for Hawk is to fill in for him with Tim when I can."

She cast an appraising look his way, but he hadn't a clue what she was trying to ascertain. After a quick shake of her head she said, "I should tell you that I reviewed the computer from your sister's friend last night and I started vetting your sister."

"And?" He crossed his arms.

"The friend didn't use his computer to access your home network and I haven't found anything to suggest your sister is involved."

"Makes me sad that they're now involved in this mess, but I get that you have to work every angle."

"I'll still need to dig a little deeper on your sister before I can fully rule her out."

"Will you let me know as soon as you finish vetting her?"

Dani nodded. "I also need to tell you that General Wilder called me last night."

Right. Here comes the thing that had her so uptight in the office.

"And?" He braced himself for the answer.

"He said they'd traced the anonymous phone call they received and it led to a disposable cell."

"So it's a dead end, then," Luke said, fighting back his disappointment.

"Yes." She braked as they approached a stoplight. "But while I had him on the phone, I got him to agree to relook at your software. Provided they haven't signed another contract by the time it's fixed, that is."

Luke swiveled to face her. "He agreed? Yesterday he led me to believe that the sabotage had pretty much ended our chances with the other committee members."

"It had, but I promised him I'd personally vouch for the software. I'll have to review it thoroughly after your team makes the corrections, but we should be able to get it in front of the committee again."

"I'm so relieved I could kiss you," Luke blurted out before his brain caught up with his emotions.

She came to a complete stop at the light then looked at him, straight and long, those luminous eyes burning into his like an infrared scope. He wouldn't have been able to pull away even if he wanted to, which he didn't. She was one of those women you couldn't seem to take your eyes off. Not because of her physical beauty, but because of a strength and determination that glowed from inside.

He wanted to ignore his common sense and give in to the sparks of interest. To forget everything else. To finally forget all about the hurtful things Wendy had flung at him before she'd left and think about dating again.

Wendy. Right.

Be a real man, she'd shouted at him. *Let go of SatCom and get a job that can support a wife and family.*

Words that sounded very much like his father's when Luke had tried out for the SEALs. He'd thought his dad would be proud. Instead, he'd cut Luke to the quick when he'd said becoming a SEAL wasn't honorable. It was selfish and self-serving. Only men who sought accolades as the hero followed that path. Real, hardworking men settled down with a wife and family.

Luke had worked even harder to make it as a SEAL after that, but he'd carried his father's words as he carried his backpack, unloading a bit of the old man's garbage with each trip.

He thought he'd succeeded in ridding himself of all of it until Wendy had spit similar words at him.

Now he got it. He still let his father's criticisms linger and he wasn't fit for a relationship. Not fit for duty. End of story.

He jerked his gaze away. The light changed and Dani eased the car forward. An awkward silence descended on them, the air thick with tension. He'd probably offended her with his kissing comment.

He looked at her and waited for her to glance his way. "I'm sorry, Dani. My comment about kissing you was inappropriate."

"It was nothing," she said, but quickly darted her focus back to the front. "I could never have worked in law enforcement for as long as I did if something like that bothered me."

Glad he hadn't stepped on her toes, he turned to watch the scenery on the Sunset Highway fly past. Traffic was heavy this time of morning, but they soon swooped down the Sylvan Hill and into the tunnel before exiting into downtown Portland.

"So the guy we're going to see is Freddy Eggleston." Dani glanced over her shoulder and changed lanes. "Ring any bells?"

"None."

"He has a long rap sheet. Served time for breaking and entering and once for assault. Nothing that would make me think he has the brains to sabotage your software."

"I'm hoping he'll at least be able to tell us where he got this computer."

"Me, too, but don't hold your breath. Criminals like Eggleston rarely offer to cooperate unless there's something in it for them."

A vision of Dani as an FBI agent sitting across the interrogation table from known felons flashed into Luke's head, and he didn't like the picture. Not one bit. "Maybe we should have the police talk to him instead of doing it ourselves."

She cast him an as-if look. "So did you have a chance last night to think about who'd want to sabotage your software?"

Wishing she hadn't so deftly changed the subject, he nodded. "Only thing I can come up with is our competitor, Security-Watchdog, wanting us to tank so they can get the contract."

She clicked on her blinker, then turned the corner into a residential area. "Since we're talking about a multimillion-dollar contract, I think that's a good possibility. But it could also be someone holding a grudge against you."

He hadn't considered that this might be a personal attack. Was there someone who'd want to set him up to take the fall for treason?

He ran though his life and couldn't come up with a single suspect. "I'm not a Boy Scout by any means, but I doubt anyone hates me enough to risk going to jail for treason."

"Still," she said. "You should spend some time thinking about it."

"I will, but I think we should look into corporate espionage right away. Though I don't know anything about the owners of Security-Watchdog," he quickly added as he hated to cast suspicion on anyone without reason.

"Already started. Two of the three named partners are IT professionals who've worked in a few big firms here in Portland, and they seem credible."

"And the other partner?" Luke asked. "Anything unusual jump out at you?"

"Before we talk about him, remember IT professionals know how software is sabotaged or they wouldn't be able to protect their own investments. That doesn't mean they have the desire to act on it, though. The other guy's former military like you. That could mean he's more likely to engage in subversive tactics, so I'll keep digging into the company."

So that's how she saw him. Military through and through. But he was so much more than that. He was kind of hurt that she didn't see beyond the SEAL, but most people didn't after they learned about his military career. Not that he'd let her know it stung. Better to make light of it. "You don't think I'd do something subversive, do you?"

She shot him a quick look of horror, and he couldn't contain his smile.

She smirked. "Oh, I get it. You're teasing me."

"Kind of slow on the draw this morning, aren't you, Justice?"

"If we find Eggleston at home, you better hope not." She chuckled, and he couldn't help but be impressed with how she maintained an even-keel temperament most of the time.

He'd been like that once. Before he'd gotten old enough for his father to bully and belittle while trying to control Luke's future. Long before his father had lost it when his mother had threatened to leave him and he'd set the house on fire, killing himself along with Luke's mother and older sister. Not a thought he'd linger on when he'd just managed to lighten his mood. He needed to be more like Dani. Upbeat. Cheerful.

"It's showtime." Enthusiasm bubbled through her voice as she turned into an older neighborhood.

He caught her mood. "You're as excited as a rookie on her first case."

"Actually this is the first investigation I've taken lead on since starting our agency." She shot out a hand. "And before you get worried because you don't think I can handle your case, I've been lead agent on many cyber crime investigations for the FBI and had no complaints."

"I'm not worried in the least," he said and meant it. But when he spotted the homes in disrepair and unkempt yards surrounding them, concern nagged at him.

Not Dani. Her eyes alight with anticipation, she eased slowly down the street and pulled up to a home with peeling white paint and a sagging front porch. A lawn covered in knee-high weeds surrounded the small bungalow. Just the kind of place a criminal might live. She turned the engine off, and he reached for his door handle.

"Wait." She punched numbers on a safe bolted between the seats, then pulled out a Glock 45 and seated an ammo clip.

His mouth dropped open when she easily chambered a round like one of his SEAL team members. He didn't know why seeing her handle a gun like a pro surprised him, but it did. "I didn't expect you to carry."

"You never know what might be waiting for us behind that door." Her focus turned deadly serious, and for the first time, he saw Dani Justice, former federal agent, and his respect for her doubled.

"I feel a little naked," he said, hoping she might have another gun for him.

"Just stay behind me and I'll protect you from the big bad man." She winked at him and her lips curled up in a grin.

He imagined this slender woman gracefully strolling up the walkway, his big, hulking body following. Seemed like something he'd see in a cartoon and he couldn't stem a burst of laughter.

"Care to share the joke?"

"Just that you're so...I don't know, fragile-looking that it's hard to picture you as my protector."

She holstered her gun with a firm snap of her wrist and met his gaze, her eyes filled with disappointment. "I'm tougher than I look, Luke. Don't make the mistake of underestimating me." She clipped her holster on her belt. "Stay behind me, and at the door stay away from the peephole while I work my girlish charms on Eggleston to see if we can get him to come out."

He still didn't like letting a woman put herself at risk for him, but he followed her up the stairs and stood to the side of the door as she directed. A quick stab at the doorbell and she stood back. The soft breeze carried her fresh coconut scent his way, making the home seem not quite as dismal.

"Hello," she called out in a sweet tone. "Is anyone home?"

Luke watched the transformation from a gun-toting, tough investigator to this very feminine woman. He suspected she'd taken down a suspect or two using her femininity over the years. He'd gladly fall for it, and he wasn't an overly trusting guy.

She smiled at him, and that now familiar zing of interest kept his eyes fixed on her. She really was something else. He couldn't help but think dating her would never get boring and wished that he was up for the challenge.

"Hello," she called again.

Luke heard footsteps coming toward the door. Whisper-quiet, though, as if the guy didn't want them to know he was home. When Luke saw the peephole in the door darken, he shot out a hand to pull her away. She deflected it, put her hand on her hip and faced the door again.

"I'm having car trouble," she said loudly. "Do you have a phone I can use?"

Luke waited, listening for any sound, especially the chambering of a bullet.

Seconds ticked by. Slow, tense, weighty seconds.

Something was wrong.

If Eggleston bought Dani's story, he should be opening the door by now. Luke couldn't abide her standing in front of the door any longer. Made her too vulnerable to gunfire. He slipped his hand around her elbow and pulled her to him.

"What're you doing?" she whispered and jerked free.

He heard a screen door slamming in the backyard.

"He's running." She bolted down the steps, and it took Luke a second to react.

By the time he moved, she'd raced through the weed-filled yard to a chain-link fence. He charged after her, nearly stumbling over a stump hidden in the weeds. She leaped over the fence, landing with the grace he'd come to expect from her. He hurdled the fence, all of his injuries from yesterday screaming at once, stealing his breath and stopping him in his tracks. When he could breathe again, he pounded around a building and into a narrow alley littered with trash.

Dani neared the mouth of the alley and he heard her shout, "Freeze."

Luke kept running, clamping down on his teeth to stem the pain as he charged over the crumbling asphalt.

"Don't," he yelled when he saw her make a diving attempt to stop Eggleston.

She landed with hands on his shoulders and dragged him to the ground. By the time Luke reached her, she'd wrenched Eggleston's arms behind his back and was sitting back, breathing deep. Luke dropped down beside her and tried to take control of Eggleston, but she glared at him so he backed off. Still, he stayed close by in case Eggleston tried anything.

"Let me go," Eggleston whined, and tried to sit up. "I didn't do nothing."

Dani pressed his face into the ground. "Then why did you run?"

"It's instinct to run from cops."

"We're not cops."

"Right," Eggleston said disbelievingly.

"I'm a private investigator, and my friend works for a computer company," Dani said. "All we want is information about a computer found in your possession when you were busted last week."

Eggleston snorted. "I tell you anything and you'll go running to the cops."

"We have no reason to do that. We just want to know where you got it."

Eggleston craned his neck trying to see Dani. "Let me up and I'll tell you."

Luke doubted the creep was telling the truth, but Dani seemed inclined to let the man go.

"You try anything," Luke warned, "and I'll come after you."

Eggleston cast an appraising eye at Luke, then nodded. Dani released Eggleston and sat back on her haunches. Luke remained crouched, ready to pounce if he needed to protect Dani.

Eggleston sat up and, rubbing his wrists, he winked at Dani. "You're mighty tough for such a pretty little thing."

Luke wanted to silence the guy, but Dani ran a hand over her hair and smiled, obviously using Eggleston's interest to get the information she needed. "You didn't say where the computer came from."

"I bought it off a homeless dude I deal with sometimes."

"Where'd he get it?" Luke jumped in.

Not taking his eyes off Dani, Eggleston shrugged.

"What's the man's name?" Dani's tone was far sweeter than Luke's had been, and it grated on his nerves that she'd be so nice to a man she'd had to tackle to the ground.

"Don't know him by anything other than Smash."

Dani looked disappointed. "Do you know where I can find Smash?"

"Nah. He doesn't bed down in a regular spot. Likes to be free, you know what I mean? But I run into him every now and then."

Dani pulled out a hundred-dollar bill from her pocket and waved it in the air. "This will be yours if you call me when you see him."

"Oh, yeah." Eggleston reached for the money.

Dani snatched it back. "Only if you call me." She dug out her business card and handed it to him.

"Then be ready for my call, pretty lady." Eggleston laughed as he got up.

"I'll count on it," Dani answered sweetly while Luke cringed.

Eggleston took off and Dani slowly came to her feet, easing out apparent soreness in her limbs as she rose.

Luke spotted blood staining her knees and elbows. "We need to get medical attention for you."

"Later." She took out her phone, stabbed a button, then lifted it to her ear. "Mitch, good. I stopped to talk to Eggleston, and he said the computer came from a homeless man named Smash. I was hoping someone there might know where I can find this Smash."

She held her phone away from her ear and Luke heard Mitch's angry response but couldn't make out the words. Luke didn't like the guy's tone, but what could he do about it?

"How was I supposed to know you were on your way to question him?" Dani snapped into the phone. "If you'd bothered to tell me, I would've waited for you and Eggleston would be sitting at home right now."

She listened, planting a hand on her hip. Suddenly she disconnected and shoved her phone into her pocket. "You could probably tell that was Mitch, and he's miffed. Kat convinced him to take time out of his busy morning to come over here and question Eggleston. Mitch's almost here and he's mad that I wasted his time by chasing off Eggleston."

Luke met Dani's gaze. "Eggleston's probably back at his house by now, so Mitch can still question him."

"He'd better be, or I have no hope of getting my sister's husband to talk to me again." She gestured down the alley. "Let's go meet him at the house."

She limped along and Luke slipped a hand under her elbow to help.

"I'm fine," she said and shrugged free. "I don't need your help all the time. I've done just fine on my own, and I'd appreciate it if you'd back off."

He held up his hands and let her take the lead. She had a stubborn streak a mile long, and if they were going to work together, he needed to remember not to push her. Hard to do when she rushed headlong into dangerous situations.

Rounding the corner of the house, he spotted a nondescript blue sedan in Eggleston's driveway. A tall man whose bulky build said he took his fitness regimen seriously stood on the lawn. He'd folded his arms over his broad chest, and a scowl drew down his face. He had a gun holstered at his side and a badge clipped to his belt. When he caught sight of Dani, his eyes narrowed and Luke knew the guy was mad at her. Good and mad.

She didn't seem to care but hobbled up to him as if approaching a sweet little baby, not an angry cop. "A simple phone call would've prevented this problem, Mitch."

The glare Elliot directed at her made Luke pull in a deep breath and step up next to her. Not that she needed protecting from her brother-in-law or would even entertain Luke's help if she did. But Luke didn't like the look in the man's eyes, and every defensive bone in his body sat up and paid attention.

"Look, Mitch," she said, not at all fazed by the glare. "I'm sorry about what happened. You know I wouldn't have stepped on your toes if I'd known." She flashed a dazzling smile that would make Luke do just about anything, but Elliot's face remained stony. "While I've got your attention, I thought I'd ask if you'd let me come down to the station and look at the computer myself."

"Really, Dani? You think I'll break every investigative rule for you just because we're related now?"

She grinned again and actually took a step closer to the guy, who looked as if he wanted to lock her in a cell and throw away the keys. "Not every one of them. Just the ones I need you to break."

Elliot rolled his eyes. "I was so not prepared to become a part of this family."

"Does that mean I can look at the computer?" she asked sweetly.

Elliot sighed. "No, but if you give me a list of things to look for I'll have someone do it for you."

"Guess that'll have to do." Her lower lip slipped out in a cute little pout, and Luke couldn't seem to take his eyes off her mouth. A very kissable mouth.

"Be careful, man," Elliot said, clapping him on the shoulder and drawing his attention from Dani. "With the look on your face it's only a matter of time before you're as connected to the Justices as I am." Chuckling, he headed for the house.

Luke felt Dani's eyes on him, but he wouldn't look at her again. Instead he watched Elliot step up to the front door and waited for him to head inside and return with information about the investigation.

Good. Concentrate on the investigation, he thought. If he could keep his focus on the threat to his company, he wouldn't be thinking about the threat to his heart who stood just a few feet away.

Carrying her gym bag holding torn and bloody clothes, Dani wound her way through SatCom's main room filled with cubicles. She smiled encouragingly as she passed curious workers on her way to Luke's office. Though he'd founded the company, his office wasn't as large and grand as she'd expected.

He was looking out the window, standing with that perfect posture she'd come to associate with him, his cell phone pressed to his ear. He didn't turn even when she dropped her bag on the floor.

That was fine with her. She was still riled up over the way he kept trying to protect her like a helpless girl instead of seeing the abilities she'd spent many years developing.

Interfering like my brothers and taking charge like Paul, she thought as she wandered to a bookshelf filled with military photos and awards. Or maybe, she was using his behavior as a distraction from the connection that seemed to exist between them.

So not thinking about that right now.

She picked up a large photo of Luke. As she'd suspected, he was something to look at in his dress uniform. The jacket tailored to his wide shoulders tapered to a trim waist. A cap pulled low shadowed his eyes, making him look even more intriguing. Next to him stood a high-ranking naval officer who presented Luke with the Navy Cross.

So he's a hero. She should've expected that. Par for the course for a man like him. Jump in. Take charge. Rescue the helpless or those in danger. She didn't need rescuing, though he kept trying when Mitch got a little miffed. She could handle her brother-in-law on her own.

"Memorizing that?" he asked, coming up behind her.

She jerked her eyes free and set the picture on the shelf. "You're quite the hero."

He looked embarrassed by her praise. "Just doing my job."

"You don't need to be so modest. The Navy Cross is a top honor."

"I'm not being modest. I just don't happen to think I need medals for doing my duty. The only reason I displayed them was to impress the procurement committee." He motioned for her to sit at the round table where he'd placed her laptop while she'd cleaned up. "While you dig into the code, I'll arrange to have personnel files brought over. Though I have to say, since we're working on a military project, I fully vetted everyone before they were hired."

She wasn't surprised to hear him defend his team. He'd likely adopted that attitude while in the military, but she couldn't be as trusting. "People change, Luke. One of your workers could have been offered money to turn on SatCom, and we have to be thorough." She settled on a cushioned chair near her computer. "Tim gave me network logs yesterday, but I'd like to have real-time access to the network."

"He wants to talk to you anyway, so I'll have him stop by when he's free." Luke sat behind his desk and lifted his phone.

She quickly lost track of his conversation with Tim as she reviewed software change logs for Crypton and discovered Luke had never made a change, adding credence to his claim of a lack of programming knowledge. Next, she delved deeper into network logins starting six months prior and moving forward. She found a login from Luke's house during the time the two of them reviewed his home computers yesterday. Neither of them connected to SatCom, so the login couldn't have come from his home unless his wireless network was hacked. With added security protocols that was virtually impossible. Which meant the log had been altered to make it look like Luke had logged in from home.

Someone had falsified the report. They wanted to make Luke look guilty.

Thrilled to have a lead that pointed to a suspect other than Luke, the next few hours flew by as she tracked the transmission through several servers. It didn't take long for her to realize she was hunting a person who knew how to hide his tracks. As she worked, something kept niggling at her mind. The hacker's pattern was familiar somehow. She'd seen the programming style before, but where?

"Knock, knock." Tim stood at the doorway, holding out a piece of paper. "Here's the login information for the network, Ms. Justice."

She swiveled to face him. "Please, call me Dani."

"And I'm Tim." He handed her the paper. "Of course you'll need to destroy this as soon as you memorize the info."

Luke got up and joined them. "Isn't that overkill?"

Dani shook her head. "Tim's right. You can never be too careful with passwords. Especially since we already have a problem."

Tim smiled his thanks at her, lighting up his face and making him boyishly handsome. "Good to talk to someone who understands tech stuff."

"Back atcha," Dani said. "My family would rather be hung by their fingernails than talk about computers."

"I hear you." Tim laughed and Dani joined him.

"I'm starting to feel like a third wheel," Luke grumbled good-naturedly.

Tim's humor faded, and he fired a patronizing look at Luke that Dani suspected was a normal occurrence between the partners. "Guess we could talk about the investigation instead. Any new leads?"

Luke nodded. "We found the computer I told you about earlier."

Tim's eyebrows went up. "Really? How?"

Dani quickly explained about Eggleston and the homeless man, leaving out her takedown of Eggleston. "I'm hoping Eggleston gives me a call and this homeless guy can tell us where the computer came from. Maybe even give us an ID on our suspect."

"That's good news, then, isn't it?" Tim's gaze drifted to her computer screen as if the talk of Eggleston had bored him and he couldn't wait to get back to a topic he loved to discuss. "How about your work here? Having any luck?"

"Maybe. I found another login to the network that occurred yesterday. At first, it appeared as if it came from Luke's house, but as I dug deeper, I found he'd used a proxy server in a long string of proxies. I'm tracking the transmission now."

Tim gave a low whistle and leaned against the doorjamb.

"I'm going to pretend I understood that." A lopsided grin flashed on Luke's face, and now that Dani was starting to believe in his innocence, she grinned up at him. She got lost in his eyes, enjoying their obvious connection, until Tim pointedly cleared his throat.

She jerked her eyes away. She was working her dream case,

and she had to let go of this hold Luke had on her. With his good looks, Tim probably had to deal with women throwing themselves at Luke all the time. She was not going to be one of those women. She focused her full attention on Tim.

"With skills like that," he said, "it's likely our hacker's done this before."

She nodded. "But why is the question. Since there's really no financial payoff for this kind of hack, I'd say our hacker was hired to do it."

"Hired by someone who wants us to fail." Tim pushed off the door frame. "He's no match for us, right? We won't let him sink us."

"Right," she answered absently as his words tickled the elusive memory that she couldn't help but feel was connected to the case. She needed to figure it out instead of standing here talking. "Thanks for the login, Tim."

She turned back to the computer, opened Crypton and started clicking through the code while Luke and Tim chatted near Luke's desk. She went deeper into the program. A line of code jumped out at her, sending her heart plummeting.

This was it. The elusive hint she couldn't put her finger on earlier. Just a snippet of code but it was distinctive, like a trademark. A trademark for a ruthless hacker. A killer. Echo, the man who'd murdered Grace Waters, Dani's friend and partner at the FBI, all because they'd tried to apprehend him for hacking a bank's website.

And threatened to kill me if we ever crossed paths again.

How had she not seen the pattern yesterday?

"Oh, no," Dani whispered as her world seemed to collapse in on her. *Father, no. Not Echo. I can't handle this again.*

"Dani." Luke looked up. "Is everything okay?"

Okay? her mind screamed as the two men watched her closely. *No, everything isn't okay.*

Feeling as if she might be sick, Dani bolted from her chair and ran down the hallway to the women's restroom.

She leaned over the sink and took a good look at her face in the mirror.

Colorless. Fearful. Terrified.

This couldn't be happening. Not when she'd finally given up on finding Grace's killer and laid it to rest.

"But it *is* happening," she mumbled, her mouth so dry the words barely slipped through her parched lips.

Echo was back and they were not only dealing with a ruthless hacker who worked for the highest bidder, but if she did her job right and got too close to him, he'd kill her without a second thought.

FOUR

Dani continued to stare at her face in the restroom mirror. She'd never expected to see Echo involved in this sabotage. Sure, he was a hacker, but one who usually worked credit card and bank fraud. He was all about the money. The sabotage to Crypton could only earn him a payoff if someone paid him to do it.

Had she been wrong about Luke, and he'd hired Echo?

She didn't want to think so, but other than Security-Watchdog, she'd found no one else with strong motive. If the government of another country had bribed Luke to listen in to satellite phone conversations, he was the worst kind of traitor imaginable.

Tell me what to do here, Father. Give me direction.

Her stomach roiled and she clutched the sink until the nausea passed. She had to eliminate Luke as a suspect once and for all, but with her obvious attraction to him, she needed another person to vet him thoroughly.

She still wasn't ready to call in her entire family as she didn't believe they'd leave her in charge of the case, so who should she go to?

Of the other siblings, the only one she could convince to keep mum about the problem was Derrick. She'd have to invoke twin privilege, which meant he couldn't share anything she said with anyone else. He'd never betrayed her confidence in the past, but he'd been far too protective since Paul, so she couldn't tell him the whole story or he might insist on bringing in the family. She'd have to give him just enough information to obtain his help. She dug out her phone and dialed his number.

"Twinkie," he answered, his sleepy voice uttering the nickname he'd given her in kindergarten.

She glanced at her watch. "Don't tell me you're still in bed."

"I had a late-night stakeout." A long yawn filtered through the phone.

A survivor of many of those stakeouts herself, she was normally understanding of sleeping late, but after discovering Echo, she'd pry her brother out of bed no matter what it took. "I need to meet with you. Now."

"Why, what's wrong?" His voice was instantly alert.

She'd have to do better to hide her dismay from him when she talked to him in person or he'd cop his big-brother attitude. Not that he was legally that much of a big brother. He was only three minutes older than she was, but he acted the big brother in every way.

"Can't a sister want to see her brother for no reason?" She forced her voice to lighten up.

"Some sisters can, but not you." There was that suspicion again.

"Okay, fine. I have a little problem and need to run it by you."

She heard him moving around in the background and suspected he was getting dressed. "Is this about the military software you're reviewing?"

"Yeah. So there's a coffee place about a mile from here." She gave him the name and location of a shop she'd stopped at this morning. "How long will it take you to turn into a human and meet me?"

"Give me thirty minutes."

"Can you make in twenty?"

"Not and look as pretty as I'm sure you'll look." He laughed and disconnected.

Despite her angst over Echo, she grinned at their long-standing joke that he was the pretty one in the duo. And he was. In a very manly kind of way, of course.

She stowed her phone, then splashed water on her face before drying it with coarse paper towels. The brief conversation with Derrick had returned some of the color to her face. A good thing, as she had to go back to Luke's office to retrieve her purse and tell him she was leaving for a bit. He'd already proved he didn't miss a thing, and he was sure to notice if she resembled a white sheet when she walked in the room.

She pinched her cheeks to add color and set off down the hall. He still sat behind his desk with Tim on the other side. Tim had propped his grubby sneakers up on Luke's pristine desk, and she doubted that Mr. Military Precision was happy about it.

When Luke caught sight of her, he jumped to his feet. "Everything okay?"

The same question he'd asked just a few minutes ago and nothing had improved since then so she wouldn't give him a direct answer. Humor was always a good way to deflect.

"I've reached my quota of staring at code for the moment." She forced out a smile. "So I'm going to run out for a little while."

He stepped around the desk. "Is this about the case?"

She grabbed her wallet from her computer bag. "Something like that."

He crossed toward her. "Something like that or it *is* about the case?"

She couldn't tell him about Echo, and yet she couldn't lie, so she'd evade. "I've gotta go. I'll be back as soon as I can."

She spun, feeling his eyes track her to the door. She heard his footsteps behind her and sensed he'd come into the hallway to watch her walk away. Only knowing him for a day, she was sure he'd made a top-notch SEAL and wished he hadn't chosen to focus his observation skills on her.

She kept going, but it took everything she was made of not to turn around to see if those razor-sharp eyes were tracking her. She straightened her shoulders and made her steps purposeful until she rounded the corner, where she sighed out a breath. Outside, she climbed into her car and glanced up at his office window. She caught him staring down on her.

Was he watching because he was guilty of sabotaging Crypton and feared she was on to him?

"He's not guilty," she muttered as she backed out of the space, but instantly doubted her belief in him. She much preferred to believe he was on her side of this case. Thinking of him as a man who would put soldiers in harm's way wasn't palatable at all.

Hopefully this would be resolved after Derrick dug into Luke's finances. He'd either prove that Luke had paid Echo, that he'd received an advance payment for the sabotage or he wasn't involved at all.

Three simple choices. All but the last one unacceptable.

Pulling onto the road, she negotiated heavy traffic to the shop. She ordered a large black coffee with an assortment of pastries for Derrick and ordered nothing for herself. She loved a cup of coffee as much as any Portlander, but the acidic drink would only add to the ache in her stomach.

She chose a table where she could see the door and took a seat. Longing to see a familiar face, she kept looking up each time the door opened. Not just any face, but Derrick's. He'd been there for her since they were old enough to communicate, but he'd stepped up his care when their parents had died in an automobile accident the summer before their tenth birthday. Having no other family, they'd entered the foster care system.

At first, they were placed together. But then on a horrible,

horrible day that still brought tears to her eyes, one of the other foster kids set fire to the house. Their foster parents decided they didn't want to continue fostering, and no one else wanted to take both of them in. So they were separated. Forcefully, as Derrick clung to her and wouldn't let her go.

After that, he'd tried everything to get them back together. As a last resort, he'd ditched his foster home and approached the lifestyle reporter for the *Oregonian,* who'd agreed to interview them and run a story. Patricia Justice had seen the article, and before the day had ended, she'd swept them into her burgeoning family and cared for them both until she and Robert had been brutally murdered a few years ago. Dani missed them as much as she still missed her birth parents. Each and every day.

She felt her eyes tearing and she looked up, seeking God's comfort to stem the flow as she always did when these memories assaulted her.

The bells above the door tinkled and Derrick entered the shop, his eyes instantly seeking her out. A broad smile lit his face when he saw her and, overjoyed to see him, she jumped up. When he arrived at the table, she forgot all about playing it cool. She flung her arms around his neck and hugged him hard.

Though they looked alike, he was six inches taller and he pumped iron. So though he was lean like her, he was rock-solid.

He held her for a few moments, then set her away and looked into her eyes. "Hey, what's all this about?"

She shrugged. "I haven't seen you for a few days, and I missed you."

He continued to study her with large brown eyes that were mirror images of her own. "I know life without me is nearly unbearable, but this is overboard even for you."

She forced out a laugh and gestured at the table. "I got a few goodies for you."

He dropped into a chair and quirked an eyebrow. "If you're encouraging me to eat all of this junk, then something is wrong."

She sat. "I felt bad for getting you out of bed."

He rubbed a hand over his wide jaw covered in stubble and watched her. "So what's going on?"

"Someone sabotaged the software I was hired to review. If the software had been deployed, satphone communications could be overheard." She made sure to keep her tone level and devoid of the anxiety that still unsettled her stomach.

He took a long sip of his coffee. "Any suspects?"

"SatCom's owner, Luke Baldwin, is the main suspect right now, though I'm also keeping an eye on their competitor." She told him about the login from Luke's home.

"Interesting." Derrick picked up an apple fritter. "Tell me about Baldwin."

She did as he chewed on his fritter. She kept to the facts so she didn't color Derrick's impression of Luke. "I was hoping you'd look into his finances."

He set down his pastry and picked up the cup. "Has General Wilder hired you to investigate?"

She shook her head. "Actually Baldwin wants to hire us to clear his name."

An eyebrow shot up. "So why aren't you bringing this before the family?"

"Can you see Cole agreeing to work for someone accused of being a traitor?"

Derrick finished chewing. "No, and I honestly can't believe you'd agree to do it, either."

"I haven't told him we'll take the case," she said defensively. "I'm just digging a little deeper to see what I can find."

He scoffed. "Right, like there's a difference."

"Let's not argue over semantics," she said, hoping to move the conversation along. "Will you look into Baldwin's finances for me or not?"

"I don't know, Twinkie." Unless he used her nickname in greeting, it usually meant she wasn't going to like what was coming next. "Something about this feels wrong. I think we should bring this to the family before proceeding."

She shook her head at her cautious brother. "Cole would veto it, and I need to do this." She sat forward, planning to take his hand, but he moved it to his lap as if he'd read her mind. Sometimes being a twin had its disadvantages.

"Look," she said. "This is the first computer case of any merit that I've seen in years. Don't deny me the chance to use the skills I've worked so hard to develop."

He didn't speak or move, proving he was as headstrong as she was at times.

"I'll continue my investigation, Derrick, whether you help me or not."

"Fine." He planted both hands on the table and his cup jumped. "But if I find any hint that Baldwin is up to something, you drop this case immediately. Agreed?"

"Agreed." She smiled at him. "I don't have to tell you not to mention this to anyone else, do I?"

"No."

"Then we're good?"

He nodded and lifted his cup.

Wanting to be sure that he understood her determination to keep this quiet, she made a fist and held it out. He groaned but lifted his fist and bumped hers.

"Wonder twins power activate," they recited together, then both laughed as they had since the eighties when they'd seen the Wonder Twins on television as part of the *Super Friends* show. From that day on, they'd continued to use the superhero duo's slogan and fist-bump whenever they formed a secret pact. As children, they went around fist-bumping all the time. Now it only came out on special occasions and usually only in private.

"So," she said, "do you think you can have something for me by the end of the day?"

He sputtered and nearly choked on his coffee. "Really? You know how hard it is to get financial records."

She grinned at him. "For most people, but not for a super-hero investigator like you."

He rolled his eyes. "I'll start on it this morning, but Ethan's nagging me to finish another project so I'll have to spend most the afternoon on that."

"What about tonight?" Her need to find Echo permeated her tone.

Derrick arched a brow and she looked away so he couldn't get a read on her desperation to find Echo.

"Look at me," he commanded, a hint of anger in his tone.

She usually ignored him when he was being so obstinate, but ignoring him right now would only make him probe deeper. She thought about happy things like Cole's upcoming wedding and Kat's recent marriage to Mitch to clear her mind, then looked at her twin.

He studied her as if she were one of the lying homicide suspects he'd interrogated during his years on the Portland police force. "You're doing a good job of hiding whatever's bothering you, but you know I'll figure it out. You'll be in a world of hurt if it's something you should be sharing with me right now."

She didn't answer. Couldn't answer without lying, and she'd never lie to Derrick. She'd simply hope that as the person who knew her better than anyone else in this world, he didn't dig any deeper and find out about Echo. If he did, he'd halt the investigation, thus ending her dream of heading it up before it even began.

She stood. "I really need to get back to SatCom."

Derrick came to his feet, too, and blocked her exit. "Don't do anything foolish, Dani. Watch your back and suspect everyone."

Telling her how to do the basics of the job was going too

ar. Even if she was hiding something from him and needed
is help, she wouldn't let him boss her around.

She crossed her arms. "I can take care of myself, you
now."

"But you don't have to now, do you? Not when you have
family of experts to help."

"I'm not rethinking bringing them in on this, so don't even
ry to talk me into it."

He took a step closer and laid a hand on her shoulder.
After what you told me, I'm rethinking my decision and
'm not letting you walk out that door until we talk about it."

"Calling you was a mistake."

"Then why did you?"

"At the moment, I don't have a clue."

He arched a brow and watched her like a hawk.

Wondering how she'd gone from hugging him to wanting
o throttle him in less than ten minutes, she shrugged off his
and. "We've been over this a thousand times. You may be
ny twin and I love you, but that doesn't give you the right to
oss me around. If you choose not to do this for me, I under-
tand. But please don't break my trust and tell the others."
he sidestepped him and marched toward the door.

"Be careful, Twinkie," he called after her.

She hurried to her car and offered a quick prayer for safety.
he knew God was watching over her, but she also knew
He'd given her abilities to help protect herself and others.
he opened her gun safe. After seating the clip and holstering
he weapon, she slid it onto her belt. She didn't need Derrick
elling her to be careful. She may need to work this case as
nuch as she needed to breathe, but with Echo in the picture,
he knew full well that taking great care was the only sure
vay to stay alive.

Wondering what was keeping Dani, Luke paced the floor
n his office and glanced out the window as he'd done every

few minutes since she'd left. He didn't like the thought of her out there on her own. She'd hinted that her trip had to do with the case, so why hadn't he insisted on going with her?

Simple. After the way she'd reacted when he'd butted in with Eggleston, she would've gotten mad at him if he'd pressed the issue. At the time, he thought that was important. But now, when he didn't know if she was safe, he'd take mad over the worry eating at him.

What if she'd gone to meet Eggleston and the homeless man?

Luke didn't know her all that well, but he did know that taking risks was part of who she was. He didn't doubt for one minute that she would meet Eggleston on her own. If he and God were talking, Luke would offer a prayer for her safety. But that hadn't helped his mother and sister, so why should he think it would help Dani?

He saw a car pull through the security booth and watched it cross the lot and park. After a few moments, Dani slid out, coming to stand on those legs that seemed to go on for miles. She brushed a hand over her hair, taming long strands softly blowing in the breeze.

He drew in a deep, cleansing breath and hissed out his anxiety. Not wanting her to know he'd been watching for her, he took a seat behind his desk and dug into his employee files. When she entered his office, he looked up and planned to act casual, but then he saw the gun strapped on her belt, and he jumped to his feet.

"Where have you been?" he spit out like a scolding parent.

Irritation flared in her eyes, but she said nothing and took a seat behind her computer. Of course she kept quiet. He'd come on like a caveman who'd dragged his woman home. He needed to back off and rephrase.

"I'm sorry for sounding like a drill sergeant." She didn't look up, so he crossed the room. "You stowed your weapon after we left Eggleston's house and now you're carrying again."

She glanced down at her gun as if surprised to see it. "I often carry when working a case." Her words were measured and flat when he'd expected anger directed his way.

"You didn't say where you went," he said, hoping she'd take pity on him and share.

"I didn't, did I?" She opened her laptop and focused on the screen. She may not sound angry, but he suspected she wasn't happy with him at all.

He took the chair across from her, bending lower to draw her attention from the computer. She gazed at him; her rich brown eyes met his and didn't hold even a hint of what she was feeling.

"I'd like to think we're partners in this investigation and that we're working together," he said, hoping to connect with her. "If you run off, how am I supposed to make sure you don't come to any harm?"

She didn't look away as he expected she might, but kept her cool gaze fixed on him. "I told you before. I don't need you, or anyone else for that matter, to keep me safe."

Deflated at her stubborn stance that he knew he wouldn't find a way around, his own irritation flared. He crossed his arms. Too bad if she didn't want him to watch out for her. If she stepped into danger, he'd live the SEAL creed. She was his teammate now. He would keep an eye on her. No matter what she said or did or how much she wanted him to back down.

"If you're expecting me to fold because of that glare you're casting my way, I won't," she said. "I've spent my life with big brothers thinking they had to keep me safe, and if I don't give in to them, I won't give in to you." The anger he'd expected earlier sharpened her words.

He needed to find a way to gain her cooperation instead

of barking commands at her. "Don't take my need to defend you as a lack of confidence in your abilities."

"Really? How else can I take it?"

"When I look at you I don't see a P.I. or a former FBI agent. I see a very soft and feminine woman. That's what any adversary is bound to see and take advantage of."

"Where *you* are exactly what you look like," she replied, then seemed surprised she'd said it aloud.

Hating that he needed to know what she thought of him, he asked, "And that is?"

"Military through and through. Tough. In charge. Not willing to take no for an answer. Uncompromising."

He raised an eyebrow. "You make it sound like those are bad things."

"Bad? Not really, I suppose. I've just seen my share of that behavior in men I've dated, and it's not something I want in my life."

For a moment, he couldn't think of anything except how much her words hurt. Was her opinion of him that important? Had she come to mean something to him in such a short time?

Nah. He may be attracted to her, but that's where it ended. After all, if he lost his company he'd be out on the streets. Not literally, as Natalie would let him live with her, but figuratively. A man without any means. He wouldn't even have enough cash to take Dani to dinner at a fast food place, much less a fine restaurant, so there would be no relationship.

Still, her comment hurt and he didn't know what to say.

"You're deep in thought." She raised a brow and watched him. "Something you want to share?"

The last thing she needed right now was to be told he found her attractive. He needed to keep their focus on the job and try to gain her cooperation, not alienate her further.

"I'll admit I can come on strong," he said, then offered a smile of apology. "I have—had—two sisters, and watching out for them became second nature to me. But in the interest of a good working relationship with you, I'll try to remember your qualifications and think before speaking in the future."

She appraised him with those perceptive eyes, digging deep.

"I mean it, Dani. I will try. You have my word. Deal?" He held out his hand and waited for her to take it.

She did, clasping her soft hand in his. A hand made for holding, not firing a gun. Frustrated by the detour his mind took when he'd just promised to tone down thinking about her as a fragile woman, he let her hand go and returned to his desk.

The SEAL creed flashed into his mind again. He was a man of integrity—his word a promise.

He glanced at Dani. She stared at her computer, her focus intense. She would give her all to this case, and he was beginning to think that meant she might even give her life for him. The thought sent a shudder through his body, and he wanted to take back his promise. But he'd given his word, and he needed to keep it, no matter the outcome.

FIVE

Hours later as Dani continued to work at the table in Luke's office, she still felt bad for stereotyping him. She hadn't been wrong. He seemed to be all of the things she'd said. But to be fair to him, when she'd blurted out her comment, she'd been thinking of Paul. She didn't know Luke well enough to lump him in the same category as Paul, yet Luke's tendencies led her to believe he would try to control a relationship.

Meaning to apologize for her rush to judgment, she'd glanced at him several times throughout the day. But every time she opened her mouth to speak, she hadn't been able to get the words out.

Why did it matter so much, anyway? Why couldn't she just let him be protective if he wanted to be? She had nothing to prove to him. It was her brothers who'd held her back for so long. And Paul. She'd never forget Paul's need to control.

She looked at Luke again. He sat behind his desk, his posture rigid, his expression closed as it had been all day. Maybe it was best if she didn't take back her comment, as it had effectively erected a buffer between them and kept her from thinking about him when she shouldn't.

Right, how's that working for you? Who're you thinking about right now?

She sighed and forced her attention back to the computer. A blinking cursor on the open window caught her attention.

A letter *H* flashed onto the screen. Then an *e-l-l-o*.

Hello? Odd. Someone was sending her a message, but now?

She watched as words slowly unfolded one letter at a time.

Hello, Dani. Impressive. I didn't think you'd get this far this fast.

Echo! He'd hacked the network again and evaded her computer security.

What's the matter? Cat got your tongue? the letters scrolled out.

She shouldn't engage him in a conversation, should she? It would only fuel his obvious need to scare her. But if she ignored him, might he get mad and take it out on her?

Trying to decide what to do, she stared at the screen. The cursor blinked like a clock. *Tick, tick, tick,* it urged her to make a decision quickly before the opportunity was lost.

Okay, be that way. I just wanted to remind you of the promise I made after I took care of Grace. I always keep my promise, Dani. Always.

She'd never forget his promise to kill her if she ever interfered with him again. Never.

Her heart thundered in her chest and her hands trembled and turned clammy. Here she was acting so confident in her abilities and not needing anyone else, then she falls apart when a simple message flashes on the screen.

But it wasn't simple, was it?

He'd hacked through several firewalls and her computer security. If he could do that, he could hunt her down and carry out his promise.

A cry of distress slipped through her lips, and she shot a

glance at Luke to see if he'd noticed. He had and was already on his feet, coming her way. "What's wrong?"

She quickly closed her computer and laid her hands in her lap to hide the trembling. "It's been a long day and it's time for me to head home."

He watched her with hawklike precision. "Let me drive you."

Honestly, she'd like nothing better than to give in and let him see her safely home. But if she did, he'd keep questioning her until she told him about Echo. Then she was sure he'd insist on telling her family. Once they heard Echo was back, they'd pull her off this case without a chance to defend herself. She couldn't—wouldn't—let that happen.

She cast a defiant look at Luke and packed up her computer.

"Don't tell me," he said sardonically. "I'm pushing too hard?"

"Yes."

"What's so wrong with wanting to make sure you get home okay after such a trying day?"

She struggled to find a good answer, and when she saw Tim pass in the hallway, an idea popped into her mind. "Tim's had a difficult day, too. Are you going to drive him home?"

"No, but—" He abruptly ended his sentence, and she could see his thoughts travel over his face.

Hoisting her computer strap onto her shoulder, she headed for the door. "I'll see you first thing in the morning, Luke."

She didn't look back, but as she walked down the hallway, she settled her hand on her weapon to assure herself that it was there if she needed it. Certain Luke was watching her out the window as he'd done earlier today, she didn't look up but climbed behind the wheel of her car. She made her way through the parking lot and out the security gate. As she turned onto the main road, she was sure she saw Luke's rental car pull through the gate behind her. She doubted he'd decided to head home this early, but surely he wasn't planning to follow her, was he? Not after his promise.

She pointed her car toward home, glancing in the mirror every few minutes and confirming Luke remained behind her. She turned off the main road onto a thoroughfare that would take her to the small town house in Tigard. She kept checking the mirror for Luke. He wouldn't have any reason to make the same turn unless he was tailing her.

His car swung around the corner. Really? His idea of remembering her qualifications was to tail her first chance he got? The nerve.

She whipped into her driveway and saw him stop down the block. Her irritation already at the boiling point, she jumped out of her car and marched down the street. At least he had the decency not to drive off when she approached his car. Instead he opened the door and slowly came to his full height. His body was obviously stiff from his injuries, but she didn't comment or offer any help. She knew by now that he'd lift those powerful shoulders into a hard line and refuse any assistance.

Just like you would do.

"Is this your way of honoring the commitment you made earlier?" she asked, her anger already lessened by seeing his obvious pain.

"Yes."

She demanded an explanation with an arched brow and pointed look.

"I promised to try and I did. I tried to watch you drive off the lot. I tried and failed." His lips tipped in an adorable smile, and despite her desire to stay mad at him, she felt her irritation melt more.

How could a man who irked her so, who was completely wrong for her, disarm her with a simple smile? She was an adult. A grown woman, who'd had her share of relationships and even survived a stalker. So why couldn't she stay mad at him?

She opened her mouth to respond, but he held up his hand "Before you say anything, this isn't about wanting to protec you. Despite your not wanting to tell me what's going on I know you've had a bad day. I can see it in your eyes." H lifted his hand as if he was going to touch her face.

She was not at all opposed to his touch, but for precisel that reason she stepped back. "I'm okay."

"That's what you've wanted me to think all day, but I don' buy it. Something's distracting you, and I didn't want it t cause you to have an accident."

His kindness made it hard to keep from telling him abou Echo. To keep from inviting him inside for dinner. To get t know him better.

"Can I take your silence to mean you aren't mad at me?" he asked.

Was she? She opened her mouth to answer when her phon chimed from her pocket. She pulled it out and saw an uniden tified caller. For a second she thought about not accepting th call and focusing on Luke, but it could be related to the case

"Dani Justice," she answered.

"Hey, pretty thing," Eggleston's slimy voice slithere through the phone.

"What can I do for you, Eggleston?" she asked, and notice Luke take a step closer as if he thought Eggleston might com through the phone and hurt her. Luke would insist she repea the conversation, so to save herself the trouble she punche the speaker button.

"I'm here with Smash," Eggleston continued. "He got th computer from a trash can in a park." He rattled off the nam of a local park.

"It's just down the street from my house," Luke whis pered as if he didn't want Eggleston to know that piece o information.

"He said he was bedding down for the night," Eggleston continued, "and he saw a dude toss it in the can."

"Can he describe the guy?"

"Just a minute and I'll check." She heard Eggleston ask Smash if he could ID the man, followed by a few mumbled words from Smash. "He says he can do it."

"So put him on the phone."

"Ah…no way. First, you come down here and give me my cash. Then you can ask him yourself."

"Where are you?" Dani asked.

"I'll meet you by Skidmore Fountain."

She was familiar with the downtown location as she regularly volunteered at the Portland Rescue Mission and attended the Portland Saturday Market, both located near the fountain. She glanced at her watch. "I'll be there as quickly as I can, but it's rush hour so it may take some time to get there."

"Be sure to bring my reward, pretty lady." Eggleston hung up.

"We," Luke said. "*We'll* be there as soon as we can. I'll drive."

Dani didn't even contemplate arguing with him. "Then let's go. We have no time to waste if we want to catch Smash before he disappears again."

They settled into Luke's vehicle and he kept his focus on the road. After the turmoil between them, Dani was glad to ride in silence. As he swung his car into a parking space across the street from the fountain, she peered through the hazy fog developing.

"There's Eggleston," she said. He was standing by the historic fountain—turned off for the cold-weather months—and wearing the same baggy jeans and hoodie, hopping from foot to foot as if trying to keep warm.

"I see him, but I don't see anyone else. So where's Smash?" Luke turned off the ignition.

"Do you think he played me to get me down here and take my money?"

"If he did, the poor man doesn't have a clue what he ha coming to him," Luke said without any inflection in his voice.

Dani flashed an irritated look at him.

He held up a hand in defense. "I'm just saying you can b mighty fierce when crossed."

She ignored the well-deserved comment and jumped ou of the car. She had to wait for a MAX Light Rail train to zip down the track before crossing the road. Luke joined her, an she cringed as the wheels grated on the metal rail's curve. Once clear, she rushed across the road. Luke reached out as i to take her arm, then fisted his hand and let it fall to his side.

Despite meeting a known criminal in a dark area of town she smiled at his self-restraint. He really was trying, and sh had to give him credit for that. She approached Eggleston.

"Well, hi, pretty lady." He leered at her.

"Where's Smash?" she asked without any pleasantries.

He flapped out his hand. "My money."

"Smash," Luke said pointedly.

Eggleston took a step back. "It's the craziest thing. I go another call about the computer."

"The same computer we're looking for?" Dani asked.

"Yeah, man. What're the odds of that?" He laughed. "Th guy made me an offer for Smash's information. It was bette than yours, but I told the guy you were on the way to offe me more."

Luke crossed his arms, broadening his shoulders. "Yo were playing him to up the ante."

Despite Luke's domineering presence, Eggleston grinned. "Yeah, man."

Luke took a step closer, and Dani knew he wanted to throt tle Eggleston, so she stepped between them. "Is that wh Smash isn't here?"

He nodded. "When I told the guy about it, he raised hi price but said he couldn't get here right away. Said he'd pa me double if I found a hiding place for Smash until he could get here."

Dani crossed her arms. "So you stashed him somewhere."

Eggleston puffed out his hollow chest. "'Course I did. I mean, double the money. Come on, you'd have done the same thing."

"*If* this guy really intends to pay you." Luke kept his unrelenting stare on Eggleston. "Did you stop to think he might be watching this corner to see who answered the call and then follow you to get to Smash without paying a penny?"

Eggleston issued a string of curses under his breath.

"I'm beginning to wonder if Smash even exists." Dani searched the area to see if anyone was watching them. If so, they had to be mingling with a group of homeless men on the corner. Otherwise, the area was deserted. Maybe Eggleston *had* played them.

"Give me the hundred and I'll take you to him." Eggleston planted his hands on his nonexistent hips. "C'mon. Pay up and you'll see."

Dani shook her head. "I'll give you the money once I confirm that Smash is a real person who saw the computer being dumped."

"Fine. Follow me." Eggleston shoved his hands in his pockets, and Dani feared his low-riding jeans would fall to the ground. He turned and tromped down the road toward the waterfront.

She and Luke trailed him into the fog clinging to the sidewalk like cotton candy on a stick. A fine mist started falling, chilling her face. She suddenly realized how cold it had gotten, and she hunched into her jacket. They moved deeper into the shadows, and an ominous feeling settled over her. Despite the cold, she unzipped her jacket and rested her hand on her weapon.

Eggleston ducked behind a small building. "Hey, Smash. I'm here."

Dani paused to listen but didn't hear a reply.

She looked up at Luke. "You think this mystery caller got to Smash before us?"

Luke's eyes narrowed. "It's not looking good."

Dani slowly drew her gun from the holster and flicked off the safety.

"Is that really necessary?" he asked.

"It's dark and we're following a two-bit criminal into a secluded area when he knows I have cash. So yes, I think it's necessary."

"Good point."

She moved deeper into the space and felt the warmth of Luke's body as he stayed close.

"Oh, no," Eggleston muttered, and backpedaled toward them. He slammed into Dani, and she could see shock blanching his face.

She raised her gun and rounded the corner. A man dressed in a raggedy jacket and jeans was propped up against the building. His head fell forward, revealing a gaping hole in the back. She caught a whiff of blood's sticky, sweet scent and saw it saturating his clothing and pooling on the ground near him.

Luke brushed past her and checked the pulse of the man she presumed to be Smash. Shaking his head, Luke rose. "We're too late."

Her stomach roiling, Dani eased closer to the body to see if she could locate any clues to the killer's identity before the police arrived and cordoned off the scene. She squatted by Smash and felt his hand. Still warm. Their killer hadn't been gone long.

Smash had been killed execution-style—likely with a silencer to keep anyone from hearing the gun's retort—then dragged to the wall and propped up. With the extensive damage, she knew it was not only a close-range shot, but if Echo was behind this, he'd used hollow-point bullets for maximum damage.

The same way Grace had been killed.

Fresh fear sent a shudder through her body. Was she up to finding Echo and staying safe? Or would he best her as he'd bested Grace?

She heard Luke moving close to her. He settled a warm hand on her elbow and helped her to her feet. "Let's call the police. They're better equipped to find this killer than we are."

She dug out her phone and thought for a moment about telling him about Echo, but she needed to find Echo and make him pay for killing Grace.

The thought of confronting such a worthy foe sent another shiver over her body. Luke took her hand and slid his long fingers between hers. The fit was warm, comforting and felt so right. Like going home for the holidays.

She moved closer to him, accepting the comfort he offered. He looked down on her, his study intense and probing. He opened his mouth, then closed it again as if he knew words weren't necessary. She needed to call Mitch, but it wouldn't hurt to draw from Luke's strength first. They stood there together for a moment, united in the tragedy.

A man had been murdered—an innocent man. And the stakes in this case had just been raised. Helping Luke was suddenly far more dangerous than she'd expected, and she might have to do something she'd never entertained—depend on the help of this rock-solid man standing by her side to stay a step ahead of Echo and stay alive.

Luke watched Dani huddle under an awning erected by the police as she answered Mitch Elliot's questions. The scent of rain clung to the air as twirling lights reflected off wet pavement, but the drizzle had stopped for now. One side of the road was cordoned off with orange cones, and a uniformed officer directed traffic around the blockage. Large lights on tripods illuminated the area, including a crime scene van with its doors flung open.

Luke's focus went back to Dani as it had over and over since the discovery of the body. The tough-guy facade that she'd displayed since she'd come into his life had fallen away. Not surprising. Seeing a man with a gaping wound would do that to anyone. Even a strong woman like Dani.

He hadn't thought twice but had taken her hand in his as if he could hold on to her and keep her safe. He'd expected her to pull away, but she'd stood by him for a few moments. Then she'd also allowed him to settle his jacket over her shoulders as she'd called Elliot, who'd promptly separated them so they couldn't compare stories before his questioning.

Elliott fired his questions at Luke first before crossing the street and surprisingly softening his stance with Dani. As he stood over her now, his face held compassion. Still, she peered up at him looking lost and frightened, and the urge to march over there and take her in his arms hit Luke like a torpedo to the gut.

Something about her got to him in a way he couldn't explain. Maybe he didn't want to explain his feelings but let them take him somewhere he'd been fighting against for a few years. But what good would that do? Dani would cross those well-toned arms and fire off the look that said she'd had her fill of guys like him. Rejection was the last thing he needed with his life crumbling around him.

Would it do any good, God, to ask for Your help here, or am I truly on my own?

He waited for that feeling that God was present and watching over him as he'd felt for most of his life, but when it didn't come, he focused on the scene. The medical examiner and a tech came out of the alley wheeling a squeaky cart holding a black body bag. The sight didn't shock Luke. He'd had his fill of body bags during his military days. He'd seen death, too. Plenty of it. But death for a cause.

Not the brutal murder of a man, for what? Money? Greed?

Just like that, his life had been snuffed out execution-style with bullets that were meant to expand and do the most damage possible. A life had ended in a moment of callous intent, and Luke felt responsible. Not responsible in that he'd ended Smash's life, but in the same way he felt about his mother and sister Hannah. If he'd been able to take his father's incessant belittling, he wouldn't have joined the military and would have been home instead of in Afghanistan when the fire broke out. He could've saved them.

The guilt of not being there for the women he loved ate at him. Constantly. A pain in his gut. Fear in his heart for his living sister, Natalie.

Would he fail her, too? Or what about Dani?

He had no business thinking she needed his protection, but after this murder, she was going to get it. The killer could come after both of them now, and he didn't care how much she argued or how much he stepped on her toes. He'd have to retract his promise for the first time ever. Protecting her was now his number-one mission.

SIX

As Luke drove nearer to Dani's home, she sank deeper into his jacket and inhaled his scent lingering on the collar. She rarely gave in and let others fuss over her, but after the shock of finding Smash's body, she'd allowed both Mitch and Luke to treat her with kid gloves.

She glanced at Luke. His jaw was clenched tight as it had been since Mitch had exiled him across the street. He was probably a mass of confusion right now. Wondering why she'd accepted his help tonight after she'd firmly shoved him away until now.

She wasn't wondering why she'd melted. She knew the killer's identity and knew he could be coming for her next. Common sense said to tell Luke about Echo. To let him take over and coddle her. A flash of Paul's face as he promised to love and care for her popped into her mind. He'd promised to be there for her when she needed him and she'd embraced it, giving fully of herself for the first time since the loss of her adoptive parents.

I can't care for you if you don't do as I say, Paul had said, his voice sounding so warm and inviting, much like an old sweater that she'd wanted to wrap around her shoulders.

Then the controlling had started.

He'd had to know where she was at all times. It was for her own good, he'd claimed. If he didn't know where she was, he couldn't be there for her. Then he'd nearly strangled her with his possessiveness, and she'd broken up with him. He'd taken her hostage. Threatened her life until her family came to her rescue. She'd only recently come out the other side.

Luke's controlling instincts were too big of a risk to take a chance on. She couldn't give in to the wrong person again.

He pulled into her driveway and killed the engine. Drizzle had resumed spitting from the sky, and a layer of dense fog hugged the ground just as it had downtown. She didn't want to get out of the warm vehicle. Didn't want to leave Luke, but she would. She had to move if she didn't want to lose herself and become the dependent woman she'd tried so hard to avoid being since the incident with Paul. She forced her shoulders back and slipped out of Luke's coat.

"Thanks for the ride. I'll see you in the morning." She opened her door.

He shot out a hand. "You can't honestly think I'll leave you alone here after what just happened."

She smiled to ease his concern. "I might have melted down a little back there, but I'm fine now."

"Regardless of your state of mind, we have a killer on our hands."

She couldn't lie to him and say she doubted it. "Even if that's the case, I'll be okay."

His jaw firmed for a moment, then he took a deep breath. "This man killed in cold blood. What makes you think if he decides to come for you that you can handle it?"

What made him think she couldn't? Her back went up more from habit than from wanting to show her strength. "I've been trained by the best law enforcement organization in the world. I have a gun and know how to use it. My home is protected by a state-of-the-art security system. I'll be fine." She jumped out of the car and marched up to her house.

She heard Luke stomping behind her, but by the time he

reached her, she'd unlocked the door, stepped inside and was punching her code into the alarm keypad.

"See," she said as she spun to face him. "My system is working, and I'll be fine."

He stood on her porch, staring at her, his expression hangdog. An urge to give in and let him take over snaked through her, but she shook it off.

"I'll see you tomorrow morning." She started to close the door.

He planted a foot inside to stop her, his face a mass of iron will like Paul's the night when he'd abducted her. She jumped back and wrapped her arms around her middle to protect herself.

Luke ran a hand over his hair, then watched her for a long moment before shaking his head and stepping back. "I'll wait here until I hear the lock slide into place."

She had no idea what had made him back down, but whatever it was, she was thankful. She closed and locked the door, then set the security system. When the lights blinked their readiness, she sighed out a breath. She was too worked up to sleep, but a long soak in the deep, jetted tub would do wonders.

She heard Luke's car start as she clicked off the entry light and the room went black. With the skies overcast tonight, a streetlight filtering through the blind slats was the only light keeping the darkness at bay. She made her way down the hall, removed her gun and put it in the nightstand. She grabbed her pajamas and robe, then headed back down the hall. As she passed the spare bedroom, she sensed movement behind her. She slowed to listen but heard nothing.

"Don't move," a distorted voice came from behind as a gun went to her head.

Despite the warning, she let out a bloodcurdling scream.

"Stop." He ground the gun's cold barrel into her temple and stood breathing hard behind her.

She froze in place. Her heart felt as if it might thump out of her chest as she fought for calm to analyze her situation.

Breathe. Just breathe. Nice and easy. In and out.

Better.

Now think.

The man felt a need to disguise his voice for some reason. Maybe he feared she'd escape and could then identify him. Or had she perhaps met Echo and hadn't known it at the time? The horrible thought of being near him sent a shiver over her body. She needed to memorize everything in case she got away and could bring him to justice.

Not "in case." You will get away.

He fumbled behind her, sucking in deep breaths and rasping them out. He smelled of perspiration and something else she couldn't identify. She could tell from where his voice originated that he was taller than she was, but only by an inch or so. She had no idea if he was powerfully built, so she didn't know if she should try to fight. She couldn't give in to him, though.

"You don't want to do this," she said, starting to turn so she could take a good look at him.

He clicked the gun's trigger and ground the cold barrel deeper. She instantly stopped moving. A rigid plastic cable tie looped around one of her wrists, and he jerked it behind her back.

"Put your other hand in," he commanded, stepping closer.

With the trigger cocked, she knew better than to fight, so she put her hand in the loop.

He yanked the cord tight, slicing the soft flesh of her wrists and binding them tight. She stifled a cry of pain. A cry of panic.

"Sit," he barked, his voice cartoonish from the mechanical device.

She couldn't sit. If she did, she'd no longer be able to fight back effectively.

Help me, God. Please help me, she prayed as she ignored the command and remained standing.

"Fine, have it your way." He kicked the back of her knees with stiff boots and she dropped to the ground.

She hit the wooden floor hard but managed to stay upright. He shoved her down with another swift kick. Pain lanced into her shoulder, but she bit her lip to keep from crying out.

Light spilled from the bathroom window, allowing her to make out a few details. He was dressed in black, a ski mask in place. A hard plastic object was wedged in the mouth hole, keeping his true voice a secret. He was on the slender side, with bulging biceps. She squinted to see if she could make out his eye color, but a shadow covered his face.

He held his gun on her while he retrieved another cable tie from his pocket.

Bending forward, he jerked her ankles together. If he managed to secure them with the cable tie, she would never get away from him, and she would die.

She had to act. Now!

He bent lower. She brought her foot up and knocked the gun from his hand. It flew down the hallway, hit the wall and slid along the floor.

The impact triggered the gun. A deafening explosion and blinding flash filled the air. She pushed to her knees, the wood floor biting in and making her cry out. She struggled to stand, but her assailant grabbed her ankles and tugged.

"No!" she screamed, and toppled like a tree in the forest. She couldn't use her arms to protect herself, so she landed with a resounding thud on her shoulder. Pain shot down her arm, and she fought her desire to cry. She'd already let this creep know he'd hurt her, and she wouldn't give him the satisfaction of hearing it again.

He cinched the cord at her ankles, cutting off the blood flow to her feet. She struggled to move but could only roll onto her side. He scrambled down the hallway, and she knew he was going to retrieve his gun.

Father, please don't let him kill me, she pleaded, knowing her only chance to escape had presented itself and she'd failed. Now this crazed man was going to kill her.

A gunshot?

One foot on the driveway, the other still in his SUV, Luke paused to listen but caught nothing out of the ordinary.

Was he imagining things because he was worried for Dani or had a gun gone off in her house?

Did it matter? Either way, he was breaking down her door if necessary to make sure she was okay. Thankful he'd ignored her demands and planned to camp out in his car tonight, he turned off the engine he'd left running to keep him warm and jogged toward the house. He took the steps to the porch two at a time.

"Dani." He pounded on the door. "Are you okay?"

He listened but heard nothing for a moment, then footsteps thundered his way. The *thump, thump, thump* was way too heavy to be Dani.

"Luke," she screamed from deep inside the house, and his heart ripped in two.

Don't let me be too late. Not again, God. Not again.

"I'm coming in," he shouted while looking for the best way in. He could put a shoulder to the door, but he'd seen the strength of her dead bolt and it could take time to break through. He grabbed a wrought-iron chair and hurled it through the porch window. He ripped the blinds from their mount and saw a man dressed in black run for the back of the house.

Luke scrambled through the window without bothering to remove the remaining shards. "Dani, where are you?"

"In the hall." Her voice shook.

She was alive! *Thank you, God,* Luke thought, wondering if his prayer had helped this time.

Ignoring the warm blood sliding down his arm from the glass shards, he ran in the direction from which she'd called. Around the corner, he spotted a light switch and flipped it up. At the end of a narrow hallway, he found her lying on her side, her back to him. Thick white zip ties circled her wrists and ankles. He glanced back, wondering if he should go after her assailant or free her from the restraints.

She drew in a ragged breath and curled into a fetal position.

Luke fisted his hands. The creep who did this to her was likely long gone by now, and Luke wouldn't succeed in capturing him. Besides, he couldn't leave her alone, and he certainly couldn't leave her tied up like this.

As he hurried down the hall, her security alarm gave off a loud whoop and settled into a noisy cycle.

"Give me your code, and I'll turn it off," he said above the din.

She rattled off the numbers, and he jogged back to the entryway to punch in the digits. He sighed out his relief when silence once again reigned. Back in the hallway, he dropped to his knees next to Dani. Her eyes were glazed with fear as she stared over his shoulder as if watching for her assailant to return. He dug out his pocketknife and reached out to free her hands, but she recoiled, her back pressing against the wall.

No. No. No. Blinding rage reared up and consumed him. He clamped down on his jaw to gain control of his emotions before he said something to make the situation worse.

"Dani," he said as softly as he could, "I'm not here to hurt you. I'm here to help."

She watched him warily, seeming moments from tears. The confident woman he'd come to know was hidden so deeply that he had to believe there was more to the situation than he could see. Sure, being attacked in your home at gunpoint was traumatic, but Dani possessed internal fortitude to over-come that.

Had this man done something to her that wasn't readily apparent? Dare he ask?

He lowered his voice as if speaking to a victim like the many traumatized people he'd encountered in war zones. "Will you let me free your hands and feet?"

Lips trembling, she nodded. Once. A bare movement as if any exertion was too much, making his heart ache deep in his chest. He slowly reached for her hands. She jerked back again, but her eyes rose to meet his and a resigned accep-tance claimed them.

"I'm not going to hurt you," he said softly. "You know that, don't you?"

"Yes."

He took her hand and looked at the delicate wrist. Raw, angry welts marred the soft skin, a heavy bruise already form-ing. He pressed the knife against the hard plastic and sliced. She drew in a ragged breath and winced in pain.

"I'm sorry," he said, hating that he was hurting her more.

He slipped his index finger between the tie and her wrist and gave it a final jerk like ripping off a Band-Aid.

She cried out again, and he saw her blood coloring the tie.

How could he have let this happen to her? He'd violated the SEAL code for the second time in hours and failed to con-trol his emotions. He'd let them get the best of him, stomping away like a little boy instead of staying where he knew he was needed. Just like he'd done with his father.

How many times did someone have to get hurt or die for him to learn that lesson?

Who had to pay?

Not Dani. Not sweet, strong Dani.

He moved to her ankles, and as tenderly as he could, he freed them. He came to his feet and held out his hands. Surprisingly she settled icy fingers against his palms. On he feet, she swayed and nearly toppled.

Enough. She needed help to walk, and he would give it t her. He slipped his arm around her back and swung her int his arms. A soft "oh" of surprise slipped out of her mouth, bu she didn't fight him. He headed for the family room, carefu not to bump her ankles against the wall. He pressed her hea toward his chest and fully intended to lay his cheek agains hair that he knew was downy soft.

"No," she suddenly blurted and pushed out of his arms She landed with a thud, a flash of pain marring her face. "I'n fine. I can walk."

Despite the desire to keep her close, he held up his hand and let her go. She crossed to the sofa and tucked her leg up, exposing her raw ankles. She started to shiver, and sh wrapped her arms around her knees.

She didn't want him to help, yet she looked defeated an he felt a physical ache in his heart. He could watch her suf fer or risk her anger from helping her. No question whicl would be better. Grabbing a thick blanket, he settled it ove her body. He sat on the coffee table and waited, hoping she' call 911. But she just laid her head on her knees and rocke back and forth.

He made the call himself, and when he hung up, she looke at him.

"You're bleeding," she said and reached out a hand, the let it fall.

He looked at the two-inch gash in his forearm where th blood had already clotted. He grinned, hoping to lighten th mood. "With all my scars, what's one more?"

She stared blankly ahead, and he didn't know what to d next. He was a man of action. Sitting here and doing nothin, was driving him crazy. If she wouldn't let him comfort hei he needed to do something else to help. Anything.

"I'll make you something warm to drink." He didn't wai

or her agreement but rushed into the kitchen and put the tainless teapot on to boil.

Anger over not insisting on staying in the house with her ad him slamming a fist into the granite countertop, the pain s refreshing as it was punishing. He wanted to see her atacker punished for his actions and wouldn't rest until he was aught. Silently he exited the kitchen through an adjoining loor. He strode down the hall and, with his shirttail, picked p her assailant's gun.

A quick look told him all he needed to know. A 9 mm veapon. Smash had been killed with a 9 mm. He pulled out he ammo clip to see if it was full, the discharge sending a licking sound ricocheting through the small home.

Had Dani heard? Hoping not, he pressed a few bullets nto his hand.

"Let me guess," she said from the end of the hall. "You're ooking to see if they're hollow points like the bullets used o kill Smash."

"Stupid, I know. You can't tell by looking at the casings, ut I needed to do something." He snapped the bullets back nto the clip. "So you think your attacker was the same peron who killed Smash?"

"It makes sense that this attack is connected to the case. I aven't made anyone else mad enough to want to kill me in long time." She flashed an ironic smile. "Unless of course ou're still mad that I outed your company to the general."

Right, a joke. She was defusing the situation with humor. le'd gotten to know her well enough to know she used humor s a defense mechanism.

The teakettle whistled from the kitchen and she spun, puting her hands out in a defensive posture as if her attacker ad returned. He headed her way, his own hands lifting. Not o defend himself but to pull her into his arms.

As he neared, she recoiled. Obviously she didn't intend to

let him help her cope with the attack, nor would she entertai
the idea of him protecting her.

"I'll get your drink," he said and left the hallway befor
he took her in his arms against her will.

On the way, he dug out his phone and scrolled down h
contacts until he lighted on Mitch Elliot's name. A wave
thanks that the cop had provided his contact informatio
before they'd left Eggleston's house washed over Luke. H
pressed Call and waited for him to pick up.

"Elliot," he answered.

Luke identified himself and gave Elliot a quick rundow
of the attack.

Elliot mumbled something under his breath. "And you'
sure Dani is okay?"

"Physically yes, but emotionally I'm not as sure."

"I can't leave my current assignment right now, but I
have a uniform there in a few minutes."

"I called 911. Someone should be on the way."

"Good. I'll call Kat. You should see her in fifteen mi
utes tops."

Luke disconnected and watched Dani gingerly sit on th
sofa. It wasn't hard to imagine how she would react when K
arrived. Fireworks came to mind as he grabbed her tea an
joined her in the family room.

"Thanks." She took the mug but didn't look at him.

He was too hyped up to sit, so he wandered the room she'
decorated in a modern style in muted colors with a minimali
feel. Crisp, clean and to the point, just like her. Something h
admired, except when it came to this case. She'd rush hea
first into finding her attacker when caution would be a be
ter approach. At least an approach that would better assur
her safety. Maybe he should call a halt to the investigatio
Or find another investigator.

He turned and looked at her. Yeah, that's what he shoul

o. Find another investigator. One whose eyes didn't melt his
eart and make him worry for her safety.

"I know that look." She set her mug on the sleek coffee
able. "You want me to back off. I won't, you know. This at-
ack doesn't change anything." The tilt of her chin and de-
ermination in her eyes confirmed she would do whatever it
ook to solve this case.

Even if he found another investigator or ended the inves-
igation, she'd go rogue and hunt down the killer on her own.
omething he would only let happen over his dead body.

SEVEN

"We need to talk about this." Luke sat next to Dani an took her hand.

She should pull free as she had when he'd tried to carr her across the room a few minutes ago. At the minimum she needed to remember how Paul had carried her throug this same space and strapped her to a chair. He'd refused t release her until she agreed to consult him in the future be fore every step she took. She'd spent forty-eight hours as hi hostage before her family had realized she was missing an beat down her door.

"What is it?" Luke asked as he slid closer.

Could she tell him about Paul? Should she tell him? She' thought she was over the trauma, but the way she'd reacte to tonight's attack proved she wasn't. Telling Luke could lea to a closeness between them that she clearly wasn't ready t experience. She had to keep her distance and concentrate o finding Echo.

She slid back and withdrew her hand. "I'm just thinkin about the attack."

"If your attacker was indeed the same person who hacke SatCom and killed Smash, what do you think he hoped t gain by coming after you?"

"To stop the investigation."

"But how does he even know you're working the case?"

She couldn't tell him about Echo, but she also couldn't
. "He has to be tracking my movements on the network."

"So he's still logging on to the network?"

"I'll have to do more digging to be sure," she answered
guely, as she wasn't certain how Echo had accessed her
mputer that afternoon.

"What you're not saying is that you don't know how to stop
m from doing it again." Luke's eyes clouded over. "And that
eans he'll keep at it."

"True, but I have leads I can follow." She hoped, anyway.
fter Luke went home tonight, she would search her com-
ter until she figured out how Echo had sent his message.

"What about the alarm system? How did he breach that?"

"He could've hacked into the alarm company's database
d retrieved my password. After breaking into the house,
 likely disabled the alarm, then reset it so I didn't suspect
yone was waiting for me."

"So what you're saying is an alarm system is of no value
ound this guy?"

"I guess not," she answered reluctantly, as she knew where
is conversation was heading.

"Then you aren't staying here alone."

She felt her usual irritation rising. "I suppose you're vol-
teering for the job of my bodyguard."

A dark, intense focus claimed his eyes. "You'll find no
e more qualified than me to have your back."

She shivered and expected to feel revulsion. Instead she
und his intensity captivating. He was a strong man. One
ho knew what he wanted and how to get it. Just the kind of
an she gravitated toward, and she had to move away from
m to keep from caving.

She got up and crossed the room, hoping physical space
ould cool her emotions. A siren cut through the quiet. She
aned out the shattered window and saw blue lights swirl-

ing in the distance. A silver SUV pulled into the drivewa
Kat jumped out.

Dani spun. "You called Kat?"

He shook his head. "Mitch did."

"But you called Mitch."

"Yes."

She crossed her arms and waited for Kat to burst into th
room as she did, charging up to Dani and planting her han
on her arms. "Why didn't you call me?"

Dani shrugged but couldn't speak. Seeing her sister in th
same room where she'd untied Dani after Paul's kidnappir
brought back the ordeal. While her brothers had dealt wi
Paul, Kat had taken Dani into her arms and comforted he
Dani couldn't let the same thing happen now or she mig
fall apart.

"It's no big deal. I'm fine." She eased her arms out
Kat's hold.

Luke cleared his throat, and Dani was thankful when Ka
focus shifted to him. He crossed the room and held out h
hand. "Luke Baldwin. SatCom Software."

Kat ran her eyes over Luke from head to toe, then sh
shook his hand. "Nice to meet you, Luke. I'm Dani's siste
Kat."

Kat transferred her attention back to Dani. "Are you real
okay? Physically, I mean."

Dani nodded. "Fine, both physically and emotionally."

Luke snorted, and Dani glared at him.

"What?" he asked. "I'm just telling the truth. You're keep
ing it together, but you're not fine."

"Which is to be expected after Paul," Kat added.

"Paul?" Luke kept his eyes on her as if he expected her
tell him about Paul, which was the very last thing that wa
going to happen tonight.

"No one," Dani said, making sure her tone brooked r
argument.

Kat stepped in between them and faced Luke. "Paul's her ⟨ turned stalker."

"Kat," Dani warned, and felt Luke's gaze burning into her. I'd rather not talk about him right now."

"Fine." Kat smiled. "Then we'll talk about selling this ouse. You may have been able to live here after one attack, ut not two."

"Two?" Luke shouted. "This has happened before?"

"It's a long story." Dani crossed her arms and gave her sis-⟨r a pointed look. "One we aren't talking about right now."

Thankfully the police siren cut though the room, making onversation difficult. Lights followed, swirling through the pen door and casting the room in an eerie blue hue.

Dani went to the door and Kat followed. They stepped onto ⟨e porch, and the brisk wind sent a shiver over Dani's body. he wanted to go back inside to get a jacket, but she didn't ant to be alone with Luke.

The officer jumped from his car, and Dani hoped Kat knew im from her time on the Portland police force so he would treamline his questioning. As he charged up the sidewalk, is intensity spoke to the dangers of his job. But when he saw ɪem, his face creased in a broad smile.

"Yo, Kat," he called. "Long time no see."

"Buddy." Kat stepped forward and shook the officer's and. "How's Vivian?"

Buddy grinned before he launched into a story about his ew wife. Dani wanted to get the questioning over with, but he knew how important camaraderie was between fellow olice officers, so she stepped inside the door and let them atch up.

Luke joined her and settled his jacket over her shoulders. Iis minty scent lingered on the soft lining, and she rubbed ⟨r cheek over it. She got lost in thinking about how differ-nt things would be between them if she'd never met Paul. ⟨ut she had and she knew what she must do.

Forcing herself to remove his jacket, she handed it back to him. "I'm in good hands now, so you can go home."

She didn't expect him to agree, so when he planted his feet in a stubborn line, she wasn't surprised. "I'll go once you promise you won't stay here tonight."

"At the risk of sounding like a broken record, I—"

He held up his hands. "I know. I know. You can take care of yourself and you'll be fine." He shook his head. "Do I need to talk to Kat or will you ask to stay the night at her house?"

Dani snorted. "Trust me. I won't need to ask. It'll take everything I've got to keep her from calling in the whole Justice clan."

"Would that be such a bad thing?"

She'd made it clear how she felt about fighting for her independence, and she couldn't believe he had to ask. "Do you want me to be pulled off the case?"

"Yes," he answered quickly and emphatically.

Surprised and hurt, she took a step back. "You don't really mean that, do you?"

"After seeing you tied up in the hallway, I'm not sure what I mean anymore." He ran a hand over his head, something she was starting to notice he did when stressed. "I don't really want you off the case, but I also don't want you to get hurt. Maybe I should look for another investigator."

She couldn't believe he was suggesting this. "I can do this, Luke, and I won't get hurt." Her voice rose with each word and she felt hysterics from the night mounting.

Kat turned to Dani, her gaze questioning. "Is there a problem here?"

Dani cast a warning look at Luke, trying to tell him to keep quiet.

"I'm trying to convince Dani she shouldn't stay here tonight," he said, ignoring her.

"Hah," Kat said. "Good luck with that."

Luke's mouth dropped open for a moment before he recovered. "Does that mean you'll let her spend the night here?"

"Oh, no, she'll be coming to my house. I just meant no one can change Dani's mind when she's got it set on something. You just have to go around her."

"Kat," Dani shouted. "He already wants to put me in a protective bubble. Don't give him ideas."

Kat wrinkled her nose and dug a business card from her jacket pocket, then handed it to Luke. "Call me anytime if you need help with her."

Dani stared openmouthed at her sister. She'd always been spunky and outspoken but this was taking it too far, and Dani planned to tell her that right after Luke and Buddy departed.

"I'll see you in the morning, Luke," she said, then turned to Buddy. "I'm sure you have more pressing things to do than watch Kat be a nosy busybody. Let's get on with my statement so you can get back on patrol."

He nodded, but she could tell he was enjoying the family feud.

"It was nice meeting you, Luke," Kat said. "Feel free to call me anytime."

Luke slipped into his jacket and glanced at Dani one last time. She didn't make eye contact with him so he would leave. Shaking his head, he hurried down the stairs and to his car. Dani watched as he backed out of the driveway. She'd gotten exactly what she wanted. So why did her stomach knot as he drove into the night?

Luke had little time to lose. He jumped from his rental car and rushed into the town house. As he raced to the stairs, he caught a glimpse of Natalie sitting on the sofa.

"You've been MIA for a long time," she said, coming to her feet. "What's going on?"

"No time to talk about it." He charged up the stairs to his bedroom, hoping Natalie didn't follow him. Even if she did,

the leg injury she'd sustained in the fire would slow her dow
so he had time to change clothes.

In his closet, he shed his shirt for a military issue mo
turtleneck, then shrugged into a warm fleece. He heard
regular footsteps approaching. He prepared for questions
didn't have time to answer if he was to return to Dani's hou
before the police officer departed.

Luke shed his shoes and grabbed a pair of warm socks a
hiking boots before settling on his bed to put them on. Nat
lie stood at the end of his bed, carefully watching him. Ha
ing grown up in a military family, she knew he was dressi
for a special event, and as much as he wanted to hide it fro
her, he didn't have the time.

Her expression filled with worry. "You're preparing f
a mission."

"Not really," he said casually. "Just a thing I need to
for a friend."

She arched an eyebrow and forced out a smile. "Just
careful, Luke. Okay?"

"I'm always careful." Boots tied, he stood and pulled h
close for a brief hug. "Don't expect me back tonight."

She leaned back and looked up at him, her eyes contempl
tive, just like their mother's had been every time their fath
had deployed. "Can I call you to check in before I go to bed

"Of course you can, Button," he said, using the fami
nickname for her.

She swatted at him as he hoped she would when he us
her nickname, creating a diversion from the stress in t
room. He returned to his closet and grabbed his E&E bag.
typical escape-and-evasion bag he'd carried in the milita
was smaller and designed for a shorter period of time tha
the bag he slung over his shoulder. Since he'd retired fro
military life, he'd bought a larger bag to take hiking and ma
sure he'd included enough supplies for three days.

Hoping Natalie would have gone downstairs, he steppe

ack into his room, but she still stood near his bed chewing n her lip. He wished he had more time to convince her that his was a low-risk mission for him, but Dani was exposed ithout him watching her house.

He tweaked Natalie's cute little nose for which she was amed. "Catch you later, sis. Be sure to lock up after me."

She lifted a hand in a small wave, and he headed out the oor. In his vehicle, he set the pack on the seat and dug out is handgun. He seated the ammo clip and tucked the gun ext to his bag. Turning the key in the ignition, he revved the ngine louder than necessary.

Felt good to let out his frustration with Dani. She didn't ant him around. Fine. He got the message. Loud and clear. But he wasn't about to leave her in Kat's care alone. If that neant he spent the night in his car outside her or Kat's house, o be it.

He roared out of his driveway, his E&E bag rocking before plunging toward the floor. He planted a hand on the pack nd hoped he wouldn't need any of the gear, but as he and is SEAL team buds had said often enough, the only easy ay was yesterday. He thought that saying far more apropos o tonight than it had been in his life for a very long time.

EIGHT

Concentrating the next morning was nearly impossible fo
Dani. She'd kept it together long enough to finish clearir
Natalie of any connection to the sabotage, put out feelers fo
any gossip regarding Security-Watchdog and track the log
from Echo yesterday to a local internet account. Now as sh
waited for Kat to call in favors to obtain a physical addres
for the user, she'd lost her focus.

It didn't help that Luke kept burrowing his gaze into he
back. Her fault, really. He was only reacting to the way she
shifted her chair to face away from his desk. She didn't war
to make eye contact with him and encourage him to talk abo
last night. As it was, she thought he'd spent the night outsic
Kat's home. He'd arrived at work wearing what looked lik
black ops clothing and appearing tired. Neither she nor Ka
had actually seen him, but then, he was trained in the be
evasive skills possible.

Dani's phone rang. When she spotted Derrick's nam
her heart sped up. He was likely calling to report on Luke
background investigation. Or maybe Kat had called the fan
ily after last night's incident. Nah, if that had happened a
of them would have charged over to Kat's house last nigh
or at the very least camped on her doorstep this morning t
block her exit.

"I'll be right back, Luke." She hurried out of the room.

"Derrick," she answered as she passed through Tara's office space and into the hallway. "You have any information on that thing I asked you to check on?"

"I take it from your cryptic question that you're in the enemy's camp?" He ended with a chuckle.

She glanced down the hall to see if anyone could overhear them. A pair of workers chatted at the end of the hallway, so she thought it best to keep up the subterfuge. "You tell me if it's enemy territory or not."

"Your guy is squeaky-clean so far." Derrick sounded disappointed, as if he'd wanted to find something on Luke. She understood the feeling of wanting more excitement in the job. "Nothing in his financials. Stellar reputation. Solid guy. I still have a few details to follow up on, but it doesn't look like I'll find anything."

Dani's heart warmed, and she instantly fought off the feeling. Despite her caution, she surely hadn't developed feelings for Luke, had she?

"Dani," Derrick said.

She shook her head over how easily Luke could distract her. "Thanks for doing this for me."

"So you're still working on their software?"

"Yes," she answered, purposefully remaining vague. "Let me know if you find anything else."

After hanging up and stowing her phone, she retraced her steps to Luke's office and found Tara getting up from her desk. Dani entered the office and Tara hovered in the doorway. Her worried expression said she didn't have good news.

"General Wilder's at the front desk," she said. "He wants to talk to you. I told him you were in a meeting with Ms. Justice." Tara nodded at Dani. "He said, 'good.' He wants to talk to both of you."

"You have any idea what this's about?" Luke looked at Dani, and for the first time today, she met his gaze. She found a healthy dose of apprehension lurking in his eyes, knotting her stomach. She shook her head.

"Tell him to come on up, Tara," Luke said.

Tara gave a solemn nod and departed. Luke crossed the room, looking darkly dangerous in his black tactical pants and mock turtleneck. She could easily imagine him on a mission, his focus not distracted by anything around him as hers was.

They waited in silence, time seeming to tick by slower than normal. Dani's dread intensified, and she could only imagine how Luke must be feeling.

Heavy footsteps thumped outside, and the general soon entered the room. Dressed in his uniform, Wilder held his shoulders straight and a leather pouch under his arm. Dani knew instantly from Wilder's tight expression that Luke was in big trouble. Luke had to realize it, too.

Still, he smiled warmly and held out his hand. "General."

Wilder quickly shook hands, then withdrew a stack of papers from the pouch. "I received your email this morning, as did all the committee members."

Luke met Dani's questioning gaze, and she shrugged.

"I didn't send an email to anyone," he said as he gestured for Wilder to sit.

"I won't be here that long." Wilder handed the stapled packet to Luke.

Luke studied the first page and a flash of anger darkened his eyes. He hurriedly flipped through the packet, then tossed it down in disgust. "I didn't send this."

Dani didn't wait for permission but grabbed the packet. She scanned the email message. In it, Luke threatened the committee members and their families if SatCom wasn't awarded the software contract. The following pages held pictures of their children and spouses engaged in everyday activities.

"This is terrible," Dani said, looking up. "Luke is a man of honor, and he would never threaten anyone and especially not families."

"I concur," Wilder replied, surprising Dani almost as much as her defense of Luke had.

"Then why are you here?" she asked.

"The other committee members don't know Luke as well as I do. They want me to cut all ties with SatCom."

"If you give me time, I can prove this—" Dani slapped the packet against her leg "—garbage didn't come from Luke's email account."

"Time is one thing we don't have." Wilder faced Luke, and Dani held her breath in anticipation of what he'd say next. "After much convincing, the committee members will entertain Crypton once it's repaired, but if anything—" he paused again and met Luke's gaze "—I mean *anything* else happens, there won't be another chance."

Luke looked crestfallen, but he didn't comment or argue, just stood there, rock-solid, and took his lumps. Dani knew he'd been trained to take bad news this way, but she wasn't. She was taught to fight for what she believed in. And it was becoming clear to her that she believed in Luke. She wanted to take up his cause and argue that the committee was being unfair, but the firm set of Wilder's jaw told her nothing she said would matter. Still, she would look into the email to clear Luke's name of wrongdoing.

"Thank you for taking the time to tell me about this in person," Luke said. "I'll see you out."

Wilder tipped his head at Dani as he exited in front of Luke. Her email dinged new messages, and she sat down to look at her computer. The first email was from a programmer at a local software company. He frequented chat rooms and remembered a former employee charging Security-Watchdog with copyright infringement. He claimed they'd stolen an idea he'd been working on in his own time.

Interesting. Stealing a guy's work meant they might be more likely to participate in sabotage.

Dani fired off a quick reply asking her friend for additional details, then moved on to the next email from Kat. She'd located the information for their hacker. The transmission originated at a company called Computer Care, located at an address in Milwaukie, a suburb of Portland.

Dani quickly plugged the company's name and zip code into a search engine. All results were for computer repair companies, but nothing for an actual company named Computer Care in Milwaukie, Oregon. Maybe the company was a shell for another company.

She opened a map program and zoomed in on the address. The street view displayed a cracker box of a house in disrepair. Not the sort of place she'd expect to find a computer business.

"Are you tracing the email?" Luke's voice came from behind.

"No, but I do have the address of the company where the odd transmission came from yesterday." She looked up at him. "The company's name is Computer Care. Ring any bells?"

"No."

"I couldn't find any information on the internet, which is odd for a computer company. We need to pay them a visit." She grabbed her jacket from the back of the chair. "And before you say something about wanting to call the police or calling my sister again, we need to act before the hacker changes location."

"Then let's go."

She arched a brow. "What, no argument?"

"Would it do any good?"

"No."

"That's what I thought." He held out his hand and bowed. "After you."

His theatrics made her grin, and as she settled into her car, her mood lifted. She expected him to comment on the fact that she chose to drive, but he simply took the passenger seat. As she made her way through town, he checked the mirrors and watched out the windows as if he expected her assailant from last night to attack them in broad daylight.

Dani doubted that would happen. Echo had proven himself to be a man who hid in the dark. Creeping through the shadows of the computer world and the physical shadows to kill his victims. Neither Grace nor Smash had likely seen him coming as she hadn't, either.

Once in Milwaukie, she turned onto the correct street and searched for Computer Care's address. Locating it, she pulled to the curb in front of the house that looked even more tired and worn than the internet picture had portrayed. She retrieved her gun from the safe, then dug out a backup she carried for emergencies and held it out for Luke. "I don't ever give clients a weapon, but with your military background I know you can handle it."

"I'm already prepared." He opened his shirt to give her a look at his shoulder holster with a 9 mm snugly settled inside.

Her eyes flashed up to his. "You're carrying?"

"What choice did I have? You won't lie low, so I have to do everything I can to ensure your safety."

She should want to yell at him for his ongoing assumption that she needed his protection, but her heart betrayed her and warmed. His world was falling apart around him, and he continued to think of her safety. She may be stubborn and independent, but a girl had to melt at least a little bit at that kind of consideration.

Still, she couldn't have him overreacting to a supposed threat and ruining a potential lead. "Promise me you won't draw your weapon unless absolutely necessary."

"You've got my word on it. But know that *I* decide when it's necessary." His voice cut like a sharpened steel blade through the car.

Though the thought of him pulling her from Eggleston's doorway flashed into her mind, she chose not to argue and climbed out of the car. She joined him on the sidewalk, where he studied the building. A strong winter wind cut down the street, sending dried leaves rustling over the crumbling sidewalk. The address in question held no signage or any indication that it was a business.

"Just as we suspected. This place looks nothing like a legit business." Luke bounded up the steps and tugged on the door. "It's locked."

Dani pointed at an adjoining alley. "Let's look around back."

She started down the alley and heard Luke running to catch up. She slowed near the back of the building and held up her hand to stop him. "Let's try to do this quietly in case someone's inside."

"Covert. Got it." He smiled like a little boy playing cops-and-robbers.

She wondered if he missed his military life. He'd said he'd left the SEALs to take care of his sister, which isn't the same thing as wanting to retire. And yet, he seemed content in his job and embraced his company's mission with zeal.

She rounded the corner and all thoughts of Luke moved to the back of her mind as she surveyed the building. Nothing out of the ordinary. The windows were too high to peer in, and a single set of stairs led to a metal door. She hurried up the stairs and turned the knob. Locked.

"We need to get inside." She searched the building for an idea.

The window to the side of the door was cracked open an inch, and an idea flashed into her head. She ran down the stairs and pointed at the window. "If you lift me, I might be able to pry the window open and climb in."

He eyed the window, then her. "I'd rather you didn't go inside alone."

"I'll unlock the door for you the minute I get inside."

His eyes flashed his distrust.

"I promise," she quickly added.

"Fine. But if you don't unlock the door, I'll get inside some-how, and you won't want me to find you when I do."

She took a step back at the power radiating from his voice and body, which seemed to quiver at the ready. He really was the finely tuned instrument she'd expect from a former SEAL. Fit. Trim. Ready to deploy at a moment's notice for some of the most dangerous assignments in the military. And study-ing him intensely like this left her breathless.

He quirked an eyebrow. "You'll need to quit staring at me if you want me to boost you up." He met her gaze, his saying he could read her every thought.

Heat flooding up her neck, she marched to the window and waited.

He joined her and wove his fingers together. "Put your foot here."

She rested one hand on his shoulder and slipped her heel into his hands so she'd face the window when he boosted her up. Planting his feet in the dirt, he lifted, his biceps strain-ing under his shirt. Thankful for her daily fitness regimen that gave her core strength to balance, she let go of his shoul-der. She peered through the dirty window at a tired-looking kitchen but found no one lurking inside. She forced the win-dow open, then pulled herself up and over the sill. She landed on a worn linoleum floor below gouged cupboards. A musty smell permeated the air, and a thick layer of dust covered the scarred laminate counters.

Not exactly the kind of place she expected to find expen-sive computer equipment. Still, she heard a fan humming down the hall, and as she got to her feet and brushed off her clothes, she wondered if it was cooling computer equipment. She itched to go snooping, but her promise to Luke forced her feet toward the back of the house.

Two dead bolts instead of one secured the building, tell-ing her there must be something of value in this run-down home. She pulled open the door and drew her gun, then silently signaled for Luke to tail her into the hallway. He followed so closely that she could hear his shallow breaths and feel the heat from his body. Together they eased past a small bathroom, a bedroom and a living room, all empty. One door remained at the end of the hall.

She crept toward it and glanced inside the room. Seeing no one, she cautiously entered. The space held a long desk, the fan she'd heard humming and a single computer. The white tower sat on the floor, connected to a flat-screen monitor.

"Looks like we found the right place." Luke turned in a circle, checking out the room as he holstered his gun.

"I expected a room filled with computers." She went to the desk and pointed at circular spots on the dusty desktop. "Looks like there were other monitors here, but they've been moved. Maybe he knows we're on to him."

"Is that possible?"

"Anything's possible, but I don't think it's likely." She seated her gun in the holster and sat down in the worn vinyl chair. "Make yourself at home while I see what I can find on the computer."

Luke headed for a closet in the corner. The door creaked open with an eerie groan as she clicked the mouse to wake up the custom-built machine. As it whirred to life, she took a good look around the room. She noticed a small black object mounted at the ceiling near the door.

"Is that a camera?" she asked, and got up to take a closer look.

"Bomb!" Luke shouted, backing out of the closet.

"It's not a bomb," she said, surprised a man whose military training would've included munitions could mistake a camera for a bomb.

"In the closet." He grabbed her arm. "Run!"

A bomb? She glanced at the closet to take a look. Before she could see anything, he dragged her from the room and they charged down the hallway.

"Faster." He tugged harder on her hand, jerking her feet into high gear.

Adrenaline coursed through her body, moving her at a speed that she didn't think she was capable of, but Luke moved even faster. At the back door, he leaped from the stoop, pulling her with him. She lost her balance, and as she staggered and tried to keep her footing, he swept her into his arms.

He ran. Hard. Fast. Toward the back of the yard. His powerful legs moving at a rapid clip despite her additional weight. She briefly thought to free herself but, not wanting to risk their lives by slowing his rhythm, she wrapped her arms around his neck and clung to him.

A deafening explosion thundered through the quiet before a concussive blast pummeled into their bodies. The hot air enveloped them with a whoosh, and Luke stumbled. He danced around trying to stay upright, but a second blast slammed into their backs and forced them to the ground.

The impact jarred Dani out of his arms. She flew through the air, then bounced and rolled until her head struck concrete, and she came to a jarring halt. Blinding pain seared into her skull, and she gasped from the intensity. As a prayer whispered though her mind, her vision blurred. A dark curtain went over her eyes and she felt herself drawn down a long, dark tunnel. She blinked hard.

Luke rolled to his knees in a seamless maneuver. He clasped her face between his strong hands. "Don't leave me, Dani. Please. Stay with me."

She wanted to. Wanted to keep gazing up at the man who was somehow becoming a vital part of her life, but darkness beckoned. She fought to keep her eyes from closing, but when the pull of darkness grew too strong, she surrendered.

NINE

Luke had never felt panic race up and over his body as in tensely as he felt it now. He'd done all he could for Dani by calling 911, and that left him feeling utterly inept.

"Get a grip," he whispered. "Remember your training. The creed. Take control. Do the hard thing. The right thing. Keep your emotions in check this time." He stared at Dani's pale face and touched her cheek. She was breathing yet un conscious.

Never had living the creed been so difficult. This wasn't a civilian laying here where he could easily remain detached. Not even a team member who he'd readily give his life for. It was Dani. Sweet, soft, stubborn Dani. It was time he realized she'd penetrated his defenses, and no matter how much he denied it, he wanted to forget about his lack of income and stability to see where these feelings took him.

If she pulls through, his mind warned.

God, please. I know I've been distant since Mom and Hannah died and I don't deserve anything from You. I just couldn't believe You'd take them like that. Please don't let Dani die, too.

He looked around, thinking—hoping—he could find something to help her. Flames shot from the house, the heat brutal. He considered moving her, but movement might make her injuries worse. He placed his body between her and the

ire. The heat felt like an inferno, but he tuned it out and
ook her hand in his. He lifted his head and offered another
rayer. God didn't need another plea to care for Dani, but
Luke couldn't just sit here. He was a man of action, and this
vas the only action he could take right now.

Sirens spiraled down the road, and Luke hoped the am-
ulance arrived before the fire department. Before long, two
aramedics pounded toward them. The first one, male. Tall
nd burly like a linebacker. The second, female. Intense and
viry. They both gave the house a quick perusal, then went
traight to work.

"Tell me what happened." The male pushed Luke out of
he way.

As additional sirens screamed closer, Luke made quick
vork of describing the bomb and the way Dani's head had
onnected with the concrete. "She's been unconscious since
hen."

The female probed Dani's head. She groaned and started
noving.

"She's coming around," the man said to his partner. "I'll
et an IV going while you monitor her vitals."

She blinked a few times, then her lids fluttered rapidly as
f she was trying to remember where she was.

Had God heard him again? Had He intervened and kept
Dani alive? Luke wanted to think so. Life was so much bet-
er, easier, when he knew God was on his side.

Dani moaned and tried to sit up.

Luke knelt at her head. "It's okay, Dani. You hit your head.
The medics are taking care of you, and I'm right here."

Her gaze flitted up to him, and she opened her mouth to
peak, then closed it. He wanted to stroke her hair, let her
now he cared, but he didn't want to risk hurting her so he
imply kept his gaze locked on hers. As the medics worked,
er eyes cleared and she was able to answer their questions.

Her voice grew stronger, but Luke couldn't relax until the
pronounced her okay.

"She'll need a scan to rule out a serious head injury," th
man said. "I'll get the gurney."

A police officer rounded the corner and stopped the medi
to ask questions before marching over to them. Luke fille
him in on the situation as a firefighter arrived and assesse
the situation. Soon the firefighter and officer called the medi
over to discuss moving Dani away from the building.

Luke didn't want her to think she was alone, so he scram
bled to her side. He couldn't look at her again while she wa
as pale as death or he would lose it. He felt her eyes on hi
as if waiting for him to speak. Instead he stared at the brigł
flames greedily licking through what had once been the roo
taking him back to the loss of his mother and sister. Not tha
he'd seen their home on fire since he'd been in Afghanista
at the time, but his worst nightmares were of his mother an
sister crying out for help and knowing he hadn't been ther
to help them.

Dani slipped her hand into his. "It isn't your fault that
got hurt, you know. I owe you my life."

"So you're a mind reader now," he said, filling his ton
with humor as he forced himself to meet her questioning gaze

She raised an eyebrow and, for a long moment, studie
him. "Doesn't take a mind reader to see the guilt written a
over your face."

He didn't want to share about his family, but he also didn
want her to think he blamed himself for her injuries when h
didn't. He ached from seeing her hurt, but given the circum
stances, he'd done his best to keep her alive.

"Actually." He paused to take a breath so he could tell
story he'd never repeated to anyone. "I was thinking abou
how my mother and oldest sister died in a fire, and I wasn
there for them."

"Oh, Luke," Dani said, her eyes darkening with his pain. "I'm so sorry. I didn't know."

"If I'd been here instead of Afghanistan, maybe…" He let his words fall off. No point in putting voice to what might have been.

She squeezed his hand. "You can't blame yourself for that. You were serving your country."

"True, but my reasons for service weren't altruistic." He let go of her hand and clamped his on the back of his neck where muscles screamed from the fall. "My father was career Navy. Ran our house like a drill sergeant. I couldn't live under his condemnation anymore, so when I graduated from high school I enlisted." He shook his head. "I didn't think about the fact that I was trading his orders for other orders. I just had to get away from him."

"That's still not a good reason to blame yourself for the fire." She reached for his hand and twined her fingers through his.

He stared at their fingers woven together. Hers as soft as fine silk. His rough from hours hiking in the wilderness and trying to stay active. They were so different yet fit so perfectly together. The warmth penetrated to his core, and he really wanted to let go of this guilt to show her he was strong. To let her know he wasn't the man his father and Wendy claimed he was.

The burly paramedic came hustling toward them with the gurney. "Time for transport, Ms. Justice."

Thankful for the interruption to process everything he was feeling, Luke moved out of the way. The police officer joined him. "I need your statement."

Luke nodded at Dani. "Once she's on her way to the hospital, I'm all yours."

When they'd settled her in place, Luke stepped to the side of the gurney. "I'll meet you at the hospital."

"Think about what I said. You're not to blame."

"Here we go." The medic bumped the gurney down the driveway.

Luke followed for a distance and his heart wrenched at seeing her loaded into the ambulance. He wanted to leave now so she didn't have to be alone at the hospital. He needed to notify her family. She'd get mad—maybe yell at him—but that would be preferable to her being all alone at the hospital. He waited until the door closed, then dug out his phone and dialed.

"The Justice Agency." Kat's strong voice shot through the phone.

"It's Luke Baldwin. We met last night at Dani's place."

"Don't tell me my sister is acting up again." Kat laughed.

"Actually, no." He told her about the accident. "Looks like she'll be fine, but she's on her way to the hospital just to be sure."

"And let me guess, she doesn't want us to know anything about it?"

"We didn't talk about it. I just thought it was time your family got involved."

"You're a smart man, Luke Baldwin."

Right. Then why couldn't he get over the guilt that his head knew was futile? "I'll be heading to the hospital after I give the police my statement. Will I see you there?"

"You can count on it. And Luke—" she paused for a long moment "—prepare yourself to meet the entire Justice clan."

Four against one. Those odds were doable. Especially for a SEAL. So why did Luke feel outnumbered as he poured a cup of stale coffee in the hospital waiting room?

He squared his shoulders to portray confidence he didn't feel, then lowered his aching body onto a vinyl chair. Pain ripped along his nerve endings, but he bit his lip and fought back a grimace. Weakness wasn't allowed. Ever. And especially not in front of Dani's tough-as-nails siblings.

Three men, strapping and imposing. One woman, petite and good-natured, yet after meeting Kat last night, he knew she was as formidable as Dani. Kat was agreeable, but the others filled the room with their unspoken anger at him for involving their sister in this mess and keeping it from them.

He'd have to win them over. Starting with Dani's twin brother, Derrick, who glared at him, doubt lingering in eyes identical to Dani's.

"Just so you know, Baldwin," he said, "I won't agree to take the case of a traitor."

"Suspected traitor," Luke said, putting a thread of steel in his voice.

"He's right, Derrick. There's no proof of his guilt." Ethan Justice, the oldest of the group and clearly their leader, watched Luke like a cat would eye a mouse. "Yet."

Derrick smirked, but Luke wouldn't let the guy know he was getting to him. He took a long sip of coffee that tasted like the sludge he'd consumed in the Navy and checked out the last brother over the rim.

Cole Justice had that whole ex-military tough-guy thing going on that Luke was used to dealing with. Maybe that meant Cole would cut him some slack or maybe, as Dani had said, he'd toss Luke to the wolves.

The group fell silent, tension cutting the air. The E.R. staff had assured them that Dani would be fine, but as he waited to see that for himself, time passed slowly. Finally a nurse entered the room pushing a wheelchair holding Dani. A white gauze bandage circled her head, but her color had returned, as had the spark in her eyes.

Kat jumped up and went to her sister. "I'm surprised you're cleared to go home already."

"She's not," the nurse grumbled. "She's leaving against doctor's orders."

Dani waved a hand. "I'm fine. My scans were clear and I can rest at home better than I can here."

The nurse snorted. "She needs to be watched all night for a concussion."

Luke stood. "I'll do it."

Derrick jumped up. "Over my dead body."

Luke stepped up to Derrick and glared at him. "I'm happy to oblige if that's the way you want it."

"Stop it," Dani said loudly, then winced.

Luke felt like a real heel for acting like a teenage boy on the playground and causing her more pain. Maybe if he got the chance later on he could kick a kitten, too.

"Could you excuse us a moment?" Ethan said to the nurse as he came to his feet.

She crossed her arms. "Hospital policy says I have to transport the patient to her vehicle."

"It'll take just a minute and then you can wheel her out." Ethan smiled, and despite her obvious desire to do the right thing, Ethan's charm won her over.

She glanced at her watch. "I'll be back in five minutes sharp."

"Thank you."

When she'd disappeared between swinging doors, Ethan started to squat by Dani, but she stood. He cast her an irritated look, but she ignored it.

"After what happened last night and today," he said, clutching her arm, "you'll spend the night at Kat's place again."

"That's to be expected." She lifted her chin. "But I won't be taken off this case no matter what you say or do."

"That's not negotiable, kiddo." Love for his sister filled Ethan's tone but still brooked no argument.

Her chin went ever higher. "I'm not your kiddo anymore. In case you haven't noticed, I've grown up and can handle myself as well as any of you."

Her siblings stared at her as if seeing her for the first time as a capable adult, but Luke had no problem seeing her that way. That is, when he wasn't seeing her as a desirable woman whom he wanted to get to know much better.

Cole pushed to his feet. "I, for one, think we're wasting time talking about this when we should get out of here and find the creep who hurt her."

"I'm all for apprehending this guy," Derrick said. "But we should discuss the merits of Baldwin's case in private before we run off half-cocked."

"Nothing to discuss." Cole fisted his hands. "The best way to find her attacker is by taking his case. Since Dani's the computer expert, she'll continue to take lead on it."

The other siblings looked at Cole, each wearing a look of surprise.

"What's the big deal? I don't believe a SEAL would betray our troops. Plus you all know I'd do anything to help soldiers, and Baldwin's software is much-needed." He issued a challenging look and no one spoke. "And there's nothing in writing that says Ethan's the only one who can decide our priorities. So, we're agreed, then?"

"I'm in." Kat shared a knowing smile with Dani, but Luke was clueless on the meaning.

Ethan nodded. "Me, too."

"Fine," Derrick said grudgingly, his fiery gaze fixed on Luke. "But if you're not on the up-and-up, we'll find out."

"We'll have no problem there." For the first time since this had all begun, Luke didn't feel as if he was stranded on a sinking island. "And thank you for agreeing to help."

Dani turned her focus to Luke. "I'll need my computer brought from my house to Kat's ASAP. I want to get started on tracing this morning's email and the video feed from the camera I saw in Computer Care." The sudden zeal in her expression equaled the look he'd seen when he'd first laid eyes on her.

With her passion for her job, he was relieved to have her

on his side and not trying to bring his company down. "So how do you go about tracing something like that?"

She wrinkled her nose at him. "It depends on so many technical factors that I won't waste time listing them."

"Can't tell you how thankful we are for that." Cole mocked a shudder. "The last thing we need is for Dani to start spouting all that computer speak."

"So true." Kat started to laugh.

"Aw, come on, Kit Kat, Dani's not so bad." Ethan paused dramatically. "If you're deaf."

Dani wasn't bothered by their teasing at all, but she smiled, her full lips tipping up and lighting her face. "They're not into computers. Except when I use technology to solve their cases and keep them alive."

The siblings laughed, lightening the tone in the room and the dire circumstances. He caught their good humor and smiled along with them.

When the laughter died down, Ethan put a hand on Dani's shoulder. "I'll go get the nurse."

Dani smiled at Cole. "Thanks for sticking up for me like that."

Cole retuned the smile, but Luke could see it was strained. "About time we let our little bird spread her wings and fly."

She frowned. "Enough with the little bird comments, okay?"

Cole held up his hands. "Okay, I hear you." He squeezed her arm, then went to the coffee bar to fill his cup.

Derrick, Kat and Dani entered into what looked like a heated discussion. Luke watched them. Kat was a brown-eyed, curly-haired spitfire. Dani was elegant and graceful. Long, lean and lanky like her twin, but they looked nothing like their siblings. Kat barely topped five feet. Ethan was stockier and powerfully built. None had similar hair coloring or matching facial features.

"We're a hard group to figure out," Cole said from behind.

Luke met the gaze of the most physically imposing of the brothers. "Just looking for the resemblance."

"You won't find it except with Dani and Derrick. We're all adopted." He sipped his coffee.

"That explains it, then," Luke said, letting the surprising knowledge settle over him.

"Gives us a bond that I think is stronger than many blood siblings." He fixed a hard stare on Luke. "You should know we have each other's backs, and if anyone tries to take advantage, we come running."

"Not sure about your bond being stronger. I'd give my life for my younger sister."

"Guess that means you'll respect my kid sister, too."

"Dani?"

"Yeah, Dani. She might try to come across all hard and tough, but her heart is soft and it can be broken."

"I'm not sure why—"

"Save it." Cole held up his free hand. "You're looking at her like most men do, and I just wanted to tell you not to mess with her."

Dani caught Luke's gaze, and she stepped up to them. "You two look like you're about to come to blows."

Luke shook his head. "Your brother here was just warning me not to break your heart."

Her mouth fell open. "You didn't?"

"Not in so many words."

"Argh." She fisted her hands. "I apologize for his unprofessional behavior. Since I'm the youngest of the family, he seems to think I'm not old enough to take care of myself. Feel free to ignore him."

Luke loved seeing the fire behind her eyes and words, and he couldn't resist teasing her. "So I can break your heart then?" He ended with a smile he knew women found charming and waited to see how she reacted.

"Go ahead and try it. I'm pretty sure you're the one whose

heart will be broken." She walked away, leaving behind her subtle coconut scent that reminded him of happy family vacations at the beach.

He watched her long legs lead her across the room with a gentle sway of her hips. She was not only beautiful but spunky and determined and had gotten under his skin. Deep under his skin. He forced his attention back to Cole, who frowned at him.

Luke would do well to remember Cole's scowling face, as Luke had no business following his feelings until he could be the man he wanted to be.

With the way things were going with SatCom, that wouldn't be soon…if ever.

TEN

Dani sat across Kat's long dining table from Luke and Derrick. At the far end of the table, Jennie sat next to Ethan, his arm securely around his wife. Next to Dani, Alyssa had snuggled against Cole the minute he'd finished his dinner. Kat took one end of the table; the other remained empty as Mitch had caught a case and had to work late.

Despite having her family surrounding her, Dani couldn't join in the conversation centering on SatCom's problem. At first, she assumed it was unease from the attack last night or today's bomb, but as she contemplated, she realized keeping her secret about Echo from her family was the source of her anxiety.

"Earth to Dani," Kat said as she poured a cup of steaming coffee. "This is your case and you're not even listening."

"Sorry." She twisted her napkin in her lap.

Instantly alert, Kat sat forward. "What's wrong?"

Dani glanced at each of her siblings. Maybe with the relaxed atmosphere after a wonderful meal, now was the perfect time to share her secret. "I have something I need to tell you, but before I do I want you to promise not to get mad at me."

Ethan frowned. "I won't promise anything like that."

Jennie jabbed him in the ribs. "Yes, you will."

"And before you say the same thing as Ethan—" Alyssa gave Cole a pointed look "—I remind you that my elbows are as sharp as Jennie's." Alyssa shared a conspiratorial look with Jennie.

"Henpecked much?" Derrick shook his head.

Ethan's lips tipped in an unexpected grin, and he tightened his arm around Jennie. "Yep, and proud of it."

Cole rolled his eyes. "What did you want to say, Dani?"

"The suspect we're seeking in both SatCom's hacking and Smash's death is Echo."

"Echo!" Kat and Ethan shouted at the same time.

"You have got to be kidding me." Derrick jumped to his feet, his chair scraping over the wood floor, then teetering and crashing. "And you ran around out there without telling us, leaving yourself unprotected. Un-be-lieve-able."

"I concur." Cole's voice was deadly calm, which meant he was royally upset.

"You all promised not to get mad," Jennie offered.

"That's before she told us we're hunting Echo." Kat shook her head. "Echo, Dani? Really, Echo!"

"Who is this Echo?" Luke asked calmly, but Dani could see his breathing had quickened even though he knew nothing about Echo.

"He's the creep who killed Dani's partner at the FBI and threatened to kill her, too, if they ever cross paths again." Derrick glared down on Luke. "Now he's back and it's all your fault."

"Derrick!" The vehemence in Dani's tone caught her brother by surprise.

After Dani's situation with Paul, Derrick was just acting protective and warning Luke to back off, but he didn't have to be rude.

"You've had it in for Luke since you met," Dani added. "You're not making this easier for any of us."

Derrick crossed his arms. "Don't try to change the subject."

"How do you know it's Echo?" Ethan asked, seeming the only focused one in the bunch.

"If everyone will calm down and take a seat, I'll tell you." Dani eyed her twin until he picked up his chair and sat. "I first suspected it when I looked at the code for Crypton."

"You've known this for days?" Luke joined her family in their look of incredulity.

"*Suspected* it for days. I didn't know it was Echo for sure until yesterday when he hacked into the network again and sent me a warning message to back off. And then last night, Smash was killed execution-style using hollow-point bullets like Grace."

Luke drew in a breath, and the disappointment clouding his eyes hurt Dani far worse than her siblings' anger. "And you didn't think it was important to share any of this with me?"

"There was nothing anyone could do that I wasn't already doing."

"Hold on there." Cole fired off a severe look that had often scared Dani as a child. "We're a team—always been a team—and a team sticks together for the good of all."

Luke nodded his agreement. "No man is left alone to fend for themselves. Ever."

"All right already." Dani held up her hands in surrender. "I got it. I just didn't want you to take me off the case. And before you say you wouldn't have, you all know you would have."

"That's right," Alyssa said. "I haven't been part of this family for long, and even I know you would've put her under lock and key."

Dani smiled her thanks at her newest sister-in-law. Besides loving the fact that Ethan and Cole had found special women who made them happy, the male-to-female ratio in the family had evened out so she at least had a fighting hope when it came to family matters. Agency business was still a whole other ball game.

The kitchen door opened and closed. Everyone turned in that direction except Luke. He wouldn't quit looking at

Dani, and it was starting to make her uncomfortable. She only hoped no one in the family noticed.

Yeah, right, like any of them ever miss a thing.

Footfalls pounded their way, and Mitch appeared in the doorway. The second he caught sight of the family, he arched a brow. "Maybe I should come back later."

Kat jumped up. "Don't you dare."

"With a look like that I know better than to leave." He crossed the room and kissed her on the cheek.

"Henpecked," Derrick mumbled as he shook his head.

Mitch spun, and Dani thought he might deck her brother. Instead he said, "Your time is coming, man, and unless you want to be hounded by all of us, I suggest you back off."

"Bad day?" Kat asked.

"The worst." Mitch ran his fingers though his hair that he liked to wear on the long side. "We can't catch a break on Smash's murder. Not a credible lead in the bunch."

Kat cast a pointed look at Dani. "You want to tell him or should I?"

"Tell me what?" Mitch focused his best interrogator's glare on her.

Dani nearly wilted. "Maybe it'd be a good idea for you to do it, Kat."

"C'mon." Kat snaked her arm in Mitch's. "I'll heat up a plate in the kitchen and tell you all about my little sister's big secret."

As Kat passed Dani on their way out, Dani mouthed, "thank you." Kat responded with a look that told Dani she would hear all about this later tonight. Based on Luke's continued stare, Dani knew the same thing was true of him, and she prayed she had the strength to withstand it.

A killer named Echo? Seriously?

With a known killer after Dani, Luke wanted to knock some sense into her and make her promise never to leave his sight. Or did he really want to take her in his arms and co-coon her from the danger? Hah, like she'd let that happen.

Derrick fixed a deadly serious look on Dani. "The safe house we discussed earlier is no longer optional."

"Fine, I'll agree to stay in a safe house at night, and I won't go anywhere without at least one of you with me." Dani crossed her arms, and that stubborn look Luke had come to know so well took over her face. "But I will be going to Sat-Com during the day. The only way to track Echo is through SatCom's network."

"Can't you access that remotely?" Luke asked.

That earned him a glare from Dani. "I could, but I also need to work with Tim to review the software, and I need to do that at the office."

Luke thought she could work around that, too, if she wanted, but not a one of them in the room possessed enough computer knowledge to prove it.

"Look. You can relax." She uncrossed her arms. "SatCom has top-notch security. The property is gated with a security guard at the entrance. The employee section of the building is locked at all times and monitored with video cameras. The only risk will be in transport, and you all are the best at that so what's the big deal?"

No one spoke, and Luke could almost feel the tension pulsing in the air.

"Let's vote on it," Dani demanded. "Raise your hand if you're in favor of letting me go."

"Only agency workers are allowed to vote," Derrick said, and when Alyssa and Jennie glared at him, Luke felt sorry for the guy. "What? This is agency business, and you've never wanted to be included before."

"Never wanted to or haven't been asked," Jennie said ve-hemently.

"Do you want to vote?" Ethan asked his wife.

"No, but I also don't want you guys to gang up on Dani like you always do."

Ethan looked at Jennie for a long moment, then raised his hand. "I say Dani can go."

Kat's hand shot up. "Me, too."

Cole raised his hand.

"I want to go on record as saying this isn't a good idea," Derrick said, the harsh glint that had darkened his eyes lessening. "But now that we have a majority vote, I'll do everything I can to make sure you're safe, sis."

"Not that I'm part of the agency, but I'll do my part, as well. I'll continue to carry, and I assure you, I will also be at the safe house when you're not in the office." Luke met Dani's gaze, and even though she never responded well to being told what to do, he wasn't going to back down.

Surprisingly she didn't say a word but simply nodded.

"That's not necessary," Derrick said, drawing Luke's attention. "We've got her back."

"Another person on her detail won't hurt," Luke replied.

"I agree," Cole said. "SEAL training qualifies him to help."

"I'm in, too." Mitch let his fork clank to the plate.

Dani flashed a smile at him. "I appreciate your support especially since I wasn't forthcoming with you."

"Yeah," he mumbled. "Don't let it happen again."

Kat rested her fingers on her husband's hand lying on the table, and a flash of jealousy bit into Luke. He wanted the same closeness with a woman that Mitch, Cole and Ethan had. But then they were nothing like Luke. They were real men, as his father and Wendy would say. With wives and the hopes of a family.

Not in the picture for you, he reminded himself, hoping it would ease the longing.

"So, Dani," Ethan said. "You'll stay here tonight. Kat and Derrick can escort you to SatCom tomorrow and spend th

y with you. I'll take care of finding a safe house for to-
orrow night."

Kat pulled her hand from Mitch's and picked up her cof-
e cup. "If you give me a list of things you'll need, Mitch
d I'll run over to your house and pick them up tonight."

"Anything else we need to resolve tonight?" Cole asked.
lyssa needs to get home to the twins."

Luke remembered the brief discussion about Alyssa's twins
at Cole had adopted. Another spark of jealousy flashed.
ole had it all. A wife *and* a family.

Dani glanced at Luke. "Since I'll be at SatCom under lock
d key, can we use the conference room to hold a family
eeting tomorrow morning?"

"Sure."

"Okay, we're done here, then." Dani clapped her hands,
en cringed, likely from residual pain from her many inju-
es. "I'll create a game plan tonight and hand out your as-
gnments tomorrow."

The Justice siblings groaned in unison, and Luke couldn't
ntain his chuckle at their unified grumble. Dani fired an
ritated look at him, so he clamped down on his lips.

"We'll look forward to that, Dani," Ethan said sarcastically.

"Hey." She wrinkled her nose at her brother. "Remem-
r all the grunt jobs you've given me in the past few years?
yback is coming."

He took Jennie's hand. "We better get out of here before
e gives me something to do tonight."

The family members got up, but Luke stayed put and
atched Dani say goodbye to her siblings. That jealousy
ark ignited for the third time. His family had once been
is close and fun-loving. Now he and Natalie were alone and
e dynamics had changed. Sure, they had fun together, but
ter Mom and Hannah had died, a current of sadness still
rmeated their lives.

Kat lingered behind and took in the chair next to hir "Thanks for keeping an eye on Dani the past few days."

Surprised that she seemed to trust him with her sister care, he smiled wryly. "I wish I could say I'd done my bes but she didn't let me do much."

"Yeah, she's like that. Stubborn about proving herself all costs." Kat met and held his gaze. "Don't let her use to push you away, okay? She needs a strong man in her li whether she knows it or not."

Interesting. "Other than the job, I'm not exactly in her life

"You will be."

He didn't know how to respond, so he said nothing.

"Just don't take my acceptance as license to hurt her. know four Justices who'll come gunning for you."

"Who's gunning for you?" Dani asked, joining them.

"Nothing to concern yourself with." Kat smiled sweetl "I was just getting to know Luke a little bit, that's all."

With a wink, Kat left the room as suspicion claimed Dan face. "What did she say to you?"

"Nothing, really. Just making sure that I understood ho important you were to her."

"Translated—she warned you not to hurt me."

"Yeah," he said, wondering if he was heading down a pa to do just that. "Something like that."

Dani started collecting the plates and silverware. "No you can see why I'm so determined to do things on my own

"I guess." He got up to help. "But honestly, I can unde stand where they're coming from."

She stopped stacking dishes to look at him. "Seriously You're siding with them?"

"There are no sides here, Dani. Everyone wants the san thing. For you to be safe." He grabbed a handful of silve ware and set it on a plate. "They hover over you because the love you."

"So you're saying love excuses everything. Even stifling me from living the life I want to live."

He jerked up his head as his dad's controlling ways came to mind. "I'm not saying that at all. My dad used love as an excuse to control all of us. Especially my mom. He was obsessive about losing her, and he didn't want her doing a thing without his knowledge."

Dani shuddered. "I know all too well how traumatic a relationship like that can be. I'm so sorry you had to go through it."

Luke let go of thoughts about his family for a moment to focus on Dani. Her breathing had quickened and she seemed preoccupied. Had his mention of his dad's obsession made her think of the former boyfriend? The one Kat had called a stalker?

Luke had wanted to ask for details since Kat had mentioned it, but Dani seemed unwilling to share. Maybe now was the time to ask.

He opened his mouth, but she suddenly shook her head as if clearing it and stepped over to him. "Do you want to tell me about what happened with your parents?"

No. He wanted to hear about her stalker, not bring up a past he'd never spoken of outside his family.

She put a hand on his arm and gazed at him. Her tender touch and compassionate look made him want to confide. But could he trust a woman with his feelings again after the way Wendy had tromped all over him? Especially a woman who had gotten to him as Dani had?

"You can tell me," she encouraged as she squeezed his arm.

He focused his thoughts on his father to keep the warmth of her hand from making him lose all common sense and draw her into his arms. "After trying for years, I finally convinced Mom to leave Dad. She tried while he was deployed. He applied for emergency leave and tracked her down. He lost it and said he couldn't live without her. Little did I know he meant he was ready to die and take her and my sisters with him."

Luke felt the horror of what his father had done rise up his throat and nearly strangle him. It took iron will to force it down before continuing. "He set the house on fire that night with everyone in it. Natalie jumped out a window. Mom and Hannah weren't as lucky. If only God had intervened."

"Oh, Luke." Tears moistened Dani's eyes.

He felt his own tears burning, but he looked up to fight them off. "Nat shattered her leg and has problems walking even now, but at least she's alive."

Dani trailed her fingers down his arm, setting every nerve ending at attention. She took his hand. Her grasp was strong, yet warm. He didn't want her to let go. Ever. But he couldn't touch her and not want more. He stepped back. "I have to say my faith hasn't been the same since. Pretty much nonexistent."

"I know what it's like to lose someone you love," she whispered, her voice filled with emotions. "And to question why God allowed the loss."

"What happened?"

She moved closer to him, and he fisted his free hand to keep from touching her. "My birth parents died in a car crash when Derrick and I were nearly ten. Then, a few years ago our adoptive parents were murdered."

"I know this may sound trite, but I'm sorry for your loss."

"Coming from someone who experienced the same thing it means a lot."

She'd suffered great loss as he had. Made them kindred souls, and he wanted to embrace their connection to see if they could erase the differences that loomed large between them. He threaded his fingers through hers, then lifted their hands to rest on his chest, drawing her close enough to smell the sweet coconut of her perfume.

He swallowed hard before going on. "Makes you want t

tect those you care about, doesn't it? That's what your others are doing. They love you and want to keep you safe."

She shrugged. "Or they just want to be in charge."

"I'll bet if they were honest about their feelings—which go on record as saying we guys rarely are—they'd tell u that."

"You're speaking from experience, aren't you?" She suddenly withdrew her hand and took a step back. "Are you as tective of Natalie as my family is with me?"

"Of course. Maybe even more so, since she doesn't have skills you possess."

Dani watched him warily but didn't speak.

"It's not a bad thing, Dani. Would you expect me to give s than my all for my sister?"

"No, it's exactly what I'd expect from you."

He opened his mouth to ask her to explain, but she held a hand like a traffic cop. "It's getting late. I need to get me sleep."

Bewildered at her sudden change, he watched her and ited for an explanation.

"I'm sure you can find your own way out." She turned d walked away.

He fisted his hand and wanted to punch the wall. They'd ared something special for a moment. Something real. mething he hadn't done in a long time with a woman. d like a puff of smoke, it had vanished, and he didn't know at he'd done to make it disappear or if he'd ever get it back.

ELEVEN

In preparation for the family meeting, Dani finished co[nnecting her laptop to the projector in SatCom's confere[n]room. It felt so good to be in charge of a case and out fr[om]under the watchful eyes of Kat and Derrick. They'd stuck[her like glue since escorting her to SatCom this morning.Dani tasked Kat with hunting down the owner of the bui[ld]ing that housed Computer Care, and she'd become engross[ed]in her computer. When Derrick went to get a cup of coff[ee]Dani had snuck out of Luke's office.

She sighed. Why couldn't she let go of this incess[ant]need to be independent as easily as letting out the sigh? S[he]couldn't simply lay it down. Not after years of fighting [her]family to let her grow up. She wanted to. How she wanted [to.]But she also wanted them to respect her as an adult and tr[eat]her as such. She'd worked too hard to let it go.

Then there was Luke. What was she going to do about hi[m?]

His admission last night that he was overprotective w[ith]his sister had confirmed what Dani already knew about h[im]and should have served as a wet blanket on the feelings [she]was starting to develop. Just the opposite had happened. [His]compassion and caring as he discussed both his family a[nd]Natalie made her want to get to know him even more. Yet [if]she did, she knew he'd stifle her. So she had to walk out [on]him before she did something she might regret.

She was so confused.

Father, I can't seem to find my way here. Please help me sort this out.

"You're supposed to tell us when you leave the room." Derrick's irritated voice came from the doorway.

Still weary from yesterday's battles, Dani looked up at him. "With the way you and Kat are hovering over me like a helicopter, I needed a few minutes alone."

Suspicion darkened her brother's eyes. "Or were you trying to meet up with Mr. Traitor on your own?"

What? She watched Derrick. Usually a kind and sensitive man, he'd been acting like someone she didn't know since he'd met Luke. He never jumped to conclusions about a client, and he never held to something that had no basis in fact.

"Luke isn't a traitor," Dani said, and instantly wondered why she felt so compelled to defend him all the time.

"Are you sure about that?" Derrick sat and propped one leg on the other.

"There's no evidence to suggest he is. Unless of course you found something in the background check and haven't bothered to share it with me."

"As far as I can see, the dude's clean," he admitted reluctantly. "But that doesn't mean he isn't smart about covering his tracks."

"Are you saying he's smarter than you? That he can hide his double dealings and you can't find it?"

"No. Of course not." Derrick crossed his arms. "If he's up to something, I'd have found it."

"So why the continued insistence that he's a traitor, then?"

He shrugged and stared at her. She knew his mind was working fast and furious, but he didn't say a word.

She leaned even closer. "It's me, Derrick. We don't keep things from each other."

He took a deep breath and let it hiss out slowly. "Guess I don't like the way he looks at you. It's no secret that he's at-

tracted to you, but come on, sis." He paused for a long, meaningful look into her eyes. "That doesn't mean you have to
pursue a guy like this."

"So now, on top of not trusting me to take care of myself,
you don't think I'm a good judge of people."

"I didn't say that."

"Then what are you saying?"

"It's just…" He lifted his shoulders in a shrug. "After Paul,
I worry about you."

The last person she wanted to talk about was Paul. She'd
given him too much control in her life already, but she had
to talk this through with Derrick. "Do you think because I
made a mistake with Paul that I can't be trusted to know when
a man isn't who he seems?"

"Kinda, yeah." He rested his arms on his knee and took
her hands. "We all worry about that."

"All, as in, you've talked about this with the family?"

"Not about Baldwin specifically, but about what happened
with Paul."

"And that's why you're so testy with Luke. You've lumped
him in the same category as Paul."

"Yeah."

She couldn't blame her brother for thinking that way. She'd
thought the same thing until she'd gotten to know Luke. But
for some reason it hurt that the person closest to her didn't
like the man she couldn't quit thinking about.

"I appreciate your looking out for me like this—you've
always had my back. But you know what? I can't really be
who I'm supposed to be with everyone trying to coddle me
all the time. In that respect, you're like Paul."

"What?" He dropped her hands and sat back as if she'd
slapped him.

"Not the stalker behavior, but trying to control my every
move." She smiled to ease his concern. "Everyone's treated
me like this since I was a teen. Don't go out for soccer, Dar-

u could get hurt. Skiing is too dangerous. You're too young
drive a car. Don't do this or that. You stifled me and left
e with nothing to do but sit home."

His face creased in confusion. "But you liked staying home
th your computer."

She shook her head. "No, I got involved with computers
cause you all didn't want me to tag along and get hurt."

"You're kidding, right?"

She shook her head.

"Why didn't you say something?"

"I did. All the time, but you guys brushed me off." She
ght back tears that threatened from the years of frustra-
n. "Why do you think I joined the FBI, then told you about
fterward?"

"Because I would've tried to stop you."

"Exactly. And I've been fighting that my whole life." She
t as if a heavy weight had been lifted from her shoulders,
ving her hope for the future. "I just need you all to back off
I can show you how capable I am."

"Now?" Derrick shouted. "When Echo is after you? No
y."

"I can handle your wanting to protect me from Echo." She
iled sincerely. "Just stay out of my personal business. If I
nt to fall for a guy like Luke Baldwin, let me. Don't inter-
e. Can you do that? Or at least try to do that?"

"Yeah, I can try," Derrick said reluctantly, then grinned.
ut I still say Baldwin is the wrong guy for you."

"Luke's not the wrong guy," Kat said from the doorway.
le's perfect for Dani."

Dani's gaze flew up to her sister's stubborn face. "So you
ve an opinion, too. Even though I've never even hinted that
vas attracted to him."

"You don't have to say it," Kat answered. "It's written all
er both of your faces."

Was it really? "For your information, Luke is totally t[]
wrong kind of guy for me."

"How so?" Kat took the chair next to Dani.

"Derrick is right." At the gleam in her brother's eyes, s[]
raised a hand to stop him from commenting. "Not about Lu[]
being a traitor, but about him being wrong for me. He's co[]
trolling and stubborn just like Paul. I doubt he'd ever sta[]
me, but all the same, I need to find a guy who's easygoi[]
and laid back."

"Easy to forget about the minute he's out of your sigh[]
Kat said. "That kind of guy would put you to sleep."

"It's my life, and I'm the one who decides who is right f[]
me." Dani met her siblings' gazes one at a time. "But to ke[]
you from worrying, trust me when I say you have nothing []
worry about. If Luke Baldwin even hints at a relationship w[]
me, I will run as fast and as far from him as I can."

A man cleared his throat from the doorway behind her, a[]
she knew by the deep tenor that it was Luke. He'd heard h[]
vehement disclaimer. She turned and fired a defiant look []
him. When their eyes met, she felt that zing of interest fla[]
to life, and she wished she could take back her comment. []
issued a challenge with his gaze, and the promise she'd ju[]
made to her siblings disappeared in the blink of an eye.

Luke couldn't keep up with the rapid-fire conversation fl[]
ing around the table. From his military days, he understo[]
the risk assessment the Justice clan was discussing, but t[]
way they frequently interrupted each other and changed d[]
rections was beyond him. They surely knew their protecti[]
and investigative business.

On the one hand, it made him feel better about Dani bei[]
involved in his case. On the other hand, it made him feel u[]
needed.

That's what he wanted, right?

To focus on his business and not get involved with

woman until he could be the man he wanted to be. Especially a woman who'd just made it clear that she would run from him if he tried.

So why couldn't he take his focus off her? Off her striking eyes? Or the way she moved like a dancer at the head of the table? Or from the silky blond hair flowing freely to her shoulders? How would it feel to slide his fingers into it, cup the back of her head and draw her close for a kiss?

"Baldwin," Derrick snapped at him. "This is your company. The least you can do is pay attention."

Embarrassed at being caught in a daydream, Luke sat up straight. "I apologize. My mind wandered."

"It's completely understandable," Kat said, humor lighting her tone.

Luke looked into Kat's eyes, alive with fun and reminding him of a little imp. She knew he was interested in Dani, and she was encouraging it. Derrick would hang Luke by his thumbs if given a chance, but what about the other brothers?

He surveyed the group. They glared at him as if he was consumed with a bad case of the plague and civilization would end if he and Dani pursued their interest. Just as she'd said. They were all protective of her.

He turned back to Derrick. "What did you need from me?"

"Dani has tasked me with doing a background check on your staff." Derrick pushed his empty lunch plate away. "And I wondered when I could get their files."

"They're in my office. You can start on them as soon as we finish here."

Derrick narrowed his eyes. "I'll—"

"Great." Dani jumped in as if she felt a need to preempt her twin. "Next up is Smash. If we can gather additional information about him, it could lead us to Echo." She looked at Cole. "Of all of us, you're the least likely to stand out in the area of town Smash frequented."

Cole chuckled. "Thanks for voting me as most likely to fit in with a homeless crowd."

Dani grinned back at her older brother, and Luke could see she had a special relationship with him. In fact, as he thought about it, she'd shown evidence that she had a special relationship with each of her siblings. That she was the family member who got along with all. Maybe the peacemaker and confidante.

So why was she running from him? Was he that bad?

"Last on my list today is Security-Watchdog. My friend confirmed they were sued for copyright infringement but won the case. Still, he said the gossip in IT circles says they're guilty."

"Copyright infringement is a hard thing to prove," Luke said. "I feel for the guy, but it could be good news for us."

Kat nodded. "If they took advantage of this guy, believing they're involved in sabotage isn't such a big stretch."

"I agree," Dani said. "I have a lot of work to do on the software today, so can someone take lead on investigating this case?"

"I'll be glad to do it," Kat offered.

Luke's phone chimed a text, and despite Derrick's lecture on his distraction, Luke didn't intend to ignore it. He felt everyone in the room watch him as he dug his cell from his pocket. He'd received a multimedia message from an unknown number. He punched a few buttons and a video started playing. On the screen, Dani, Kat and Derrick arrived at Kat's house and entered the front door. A few frames later, the video showed a masked man standing in the same spot smiling up into the camera.

Echo!

He'd found Kat's house, and if the time stamp on the video was correct, he'd stood on the stoop as they'd all slept unaware.

Not knowing how he was going to tell Dani about this ad-

litional evidence that said Echo was a worthy foe, he looked
t her.

"What is it?" she asked. "What's wrong?"

He forced his apprehension aside and handed his phone
o her but said nothing. She looked at the screen, and as the
video played, her face blanched. She grabbed the back of the
hair with her free hand. That now familiar urge to sweep her
nto his arms and offer his protection doubled, but he fisted
is hands under the table instead.

Derrick jumped to his feet and snatched the phone from
er hands. He played the video and looked up, anger burn-
ng in his eyes. "Echo knew where Dani spent the night." He
anded the phone to Ethan, who shared it with Cole and Kat.
He obviously hacked into Kat's security system to retrieve
his video. The last bit is time-stamped at 3:00 a.m."

"This's a warning to back off." Dani planted her other
and on the chair. "He wants me to know that he can get to
ne even with all of you nearby."

"That's not going to happen," Derrick said with vehe-
nence.

For the first time since Luke had met Dani's brother, Luke
greed with him, but he wasn't sure how they were going to
ull it off.

"What I don't get—" Kat set down her cup "—is how he
acked my system. Dani set it up, and that means this guy
as to be as good as or better than she is."

Luke's gut clenched. If Echo could best Dani, then how
vere they going to keep her safe?

"I'd have to look at your computer to see how he did it,"
Dani said. "And I'm sure none of you are going to let me go
ack to Kat's house to do that."

"You got that right," Ethan said. "We now know who we're
lealing with, and we won't let him get this close again."

The others nodded their agreement. They were circling
around Dani like Luke would do with Natalie. Even with Da-

ni's family on guard, he wouldn't sit back and relax. He'd be at that safe house, too. But first he needed to find out how to stop Echo, and that meant understanding how he could hack into the video feed in the first place.

When the meeting broke up, he phoned Tim and asked him to come to his office. While he waited for Tim, Luke stared out the window. The sun hung behind clouds, mimicking his mood. He stretched the muscles in his neck and shoulders stiff from the night spent on Kat's sofa. Despite Dani's continued attitude, with whatever had sent her running from him last night and her protests about him staying the night, he'd had little difficulty convincing Kat to let him stay. If he had he would've spent the night in his car again.

"You wanted to see me?" Tim's voice came from behind

Luke let out a long breath and motioned for Tim to sit. He slouched in a chair and propped stained athletic shoes on Luke's polished desk. He wore baggy jeans and a wrinkled T-shirt, as he did most every day. His hair looked as if he'd just tumbled out of bed, and likely he had.

Luke didn't like Tim's sloppy ways, but then not everyone lived under the military precision he'd been raised with. He took the seat behind his desk, his gut continuing to churn over the video. "I need to know how someone could hack into video from a security system."

Tim crossed his ankles. "Someone hack our security?"

"No. A friend's system at home."

"How'd your friend know they'd been hacked?"

"The creep sent a clip from the video feed." Luke shook his head. "And I want to make sure he can't do the same thing again."

"Most often it's a matter of the network not being secure."

"Dani secured the system."

"Man." Tim shook his head, then ran his fingers through long hair. "If he could break through Dani's security, then he's good—crazy good." Tim's tone was filled with admiration for this creep, and it riled Luke.

"Tell me how to stop him," he said more harshly than Tim deserved.

"You can't, man. If the dude wants to do it again, you're not likely going to stop him."

"But Dani—"

"Dani, nothing. Don't get me wrong, she's good at what she does, but hackers spend their life finding ways around security measures she thinks up. No system is one hundred percent secure."

Luke's lunch churned in his stomach. How was he going to keep Dani safe? He was so out of his element here. Give him a visible target. Something, someone he could see. Not this whisper of attack hidden behind walls of the cyber world that Luke had no skills to deal with.

Dani packed up her computer under Luke's watchful eye. She'd spent the afternoon proving the email to the procurement committee was a spoofed email and then tracking Echo's movements but not coming up with anything new. Derrick had gone to get the car for their trip to the safe house, and Kat had made a quick trip to the restroom, leaving Dani alone with Luke for the first time since he'd received the video.

Even now, the thought of Echo on Kat's doorstep had Dani uneasy. Not one of them had expected Echo to find her. Not one of them was prepared for his arrival last night. And not one of them could have prevented him from entering the house and getting off at least one lethal shot before someone retaliated.

She'd underestimated Echo's abilities. They all had. Something she couldn't do again if she didn't want someone to get hurt.

She zipped up her computer bag, and with nothing left to keep her hands busy, she looked up. Luke jerked his gaze away as if he didn't want her to know he'd been looking at her. His phone rang and he grabbed it from his desk.

She watched him out of the corner of her eye as he listened intently. As intently as everything else he did. He hadn't been singling her out for his focus. That's just how he lived. A man of passion and excellence. Of honor and compassion. She'd seen all these characteristics in him, and yet she wanted to focus only on the part of him that frustrated her.

You have to keep up the wall. How else will you protect your heart?

"You're sure," he said loudly. His brows knit together in concern. "We'll need to call the police, then."

The police? Her heart skipped a beat. She forgot all about their differences and listened to see if she could determine what had happened now.

He didn't say another word, clicked off his phone and slipped it into his pocket. He went back to working on the paper in front of him. Not a word about the phone call. Right. Just when she began to think of his other attributes, he shut her out. He expected her to tell him everything about the case while he kept things close to the vest.

She crossed the room and waited for him to look up. "Why do you need to call the police?"

He'd turned to stare out the window, and she saw his hands clench on the arms of his chair.

"The police?" she asked more pointedly this time.

"Does your agency deal with attempted murder?" His tone was relaxed. Casual. As if he could ask such a startling question and not arouse her suspicions.

"I'm guessing this has to do with the case." She approached him and waited for him to face her.

"That was my mechanic," he said, meeting her gaze again, his eyes dark with concern. "He's finally gotten around to looking at my brakes. They didn't fail accidentally. They were tampered with. My car crash wasn't an accident after all."

TWELVE

"Who would want to tamper with Luke's brakes?" Kat asked from the backseat of Derrick's SUV on the way to Cole's beach house. Derrick and Cole thought moving Dani out of town might be safer than a local safe house as Echo couldn't follow them through the mountains without them seeing him.

"I've been asking myself the same question since Luke's mechanic called," Dani said.

Kat sat forward. "Did you ask him about it?"

"Yeah. The only explanation we could come up with is that Echo wanted to keep Luke from showing up at the meeting and somehow saving the day."

Kat nodded. "Makes sense if Echo was hired to tank Sat-Com."

"If you can come up with a better explanation, I'm all ears."

"I'll think about it." Kat yawned. "That is if I can stay awake for the next hour. This drive always makes me sleepy."

"Good thing we've got Derrick here to chauffeur us." Dani dug out her laptop. "While you snooze, I can get some work done."

Dani opened her computer and spent the next hour looking for additional leads. Derrick and Kat chatted about Luke's brakes, but neither of them came up with a better explanation.

When they arrived at the beach house and Dani saw Cole's and Luke's cars in the driveway, she knew she needed a break from everyone's intense study before they sat down to dinner

"I'm going downstairs to read for a while," she announced as she joined them in the family room, and didn't give them time to argue but headed for the stairs.

Luke jumped to his feet. "I'll go with you."

Planning to tell him she needed to be alone, she turned. She caught Derrick's look of utter consternation. He fisted his hands and opened his mouth several times, then snapped it firmly closed. Despite her angst, she had to smile. He'd tried so hard since their talk to ease up and ask instead of telling, even warning the others to do the same thing, that she couldn't tell Luke to stay here and ruin the effort Derrick had put in

"Thanks," she whispered in her brother's ear. "I know this is hard for you." She squeezed his arm and, still smiling, she headed for the daylight basement.

Thank you, Father, for opening Derrick's eyes to my needs.

Her brother truly loved her, and she was thrilled to see him try to change for her. Gave her hope that maybe Luke could change, too.

"Care to share what's making you smile?" Luke asked as he joined her in the rec room.

She settled on a slipcovered sofa and tucked her feet up under her legs. "I talked to Derrick about the way my family babies me, and he's trying so hard not to interfere in my life."

Luke took a seat in an oversize chair. "I wondered about that when I saw him being more accommodating tonight. Sounds like he's really taken your wishes to heart."

She nodded. "It's obviously hard for him to do, but I really appreciate that he's trying."

"You never mentioned if there's a reason he's so protective." Luke slid forward and planted his elbows on his knees.

"He's always stuck up for me. You know…the way a brother does. But he changed when our parents died in the car crash. We were just kids." She took a deep breath to fight back the horror of the night that could still bring tears to her eyes.

"Sounds just like my relationship with Natalie except we were much older when we lost our family."

She nodded. "Unfortunately we were too young to be on our own and we didn't have any other family, so we were sent to foster care." She told Luke about their time in foster care and the way Derrick had involved the newspaper in their plight.

Luke smiled wryly. "I have to admit I haven't much liked Derrick until now."

She nodded her understanding. "He's been terse with you, but he's a great guy."

"I get that he's protective of you, but is he like this with all the clients?"

Only the ones I want to let go of my common sense with and date.

"No, just you. Apparently the attraction between us isn't a secret." It felt so good to get this subject out in the open and admit her interest in him.

"I'm sorry if that's caused you any discomfort with your family."

She shrugged. "I can handle it, but you have to know I don't have room in my life for a relationship right now."

He dropped to his knees in front of her and looked her in the eyes. "Trust me. If I could change these feelings, I would. In a heartbeat."

At his veracity, she slid back. She should be happy about his admission. She felt the same way, but hearing it spoken aloud hurt far more than she thought it would. She didn't know why he didn't want to care for her, and she wasn't going to ask or the unexpected tears that were suddenly threatening would flow. She wouldn't break down in front of him. "Like I said. I don't need the complication of a relationship. Especially not after my last one."

"Was it with the guy Kat called a stalker?" Luke eased closer, his eyes filling with concern. "Did he really stalk you?"

She nodded.

"What happened?"

"I simply misjudged him. Paul was a great guy at first, but after we got serious, he turned controlling and manipulative. When I broke up with him, he hounded me at all hours of the night. Followed me everywhere."

Anger flashed on Luke's face. "And your brothers couldn't do anything about that?"

"They could have if I'd told them."

He sat back on his heels. "Ah, another time you wanted to be independent, huh?"

"Until he started to get physically threatening. He broke down the front door of my house. Put a knife to my throat and carried me across the living room to a chair, then tied me to it."

Luke watched her for a moment. "That's why you freaked out when I tried to carry you to the sofa, right?"

She nodded as the memory, still fresher than she wanted to admit, washed over her and those unshed tears started rolling down her cheek.

Luke reached out and brushed them away with his thumb. "Now I can see why everyone's so protective of you. If a man held my sister at knifepoint, he may not be alive to tell about it."

Their eyes met. His went dark. Dangerous and compelling. The intensity should remind her of Paul and scare her away. Instead Luke's loyalty to his sister and his fierce willingness to defend those in need drew her closer to him.

"Your sister is lucky to have you."

"I won't let anything bad happen to you, either," he whispered. "I promise." He trailed a finger down her face and under her chin.

Shivers traveled over her body. She wanted to give in. To let this man protect her from Echo. From every bad thing in life. To be a rock that she could depend on. And then what? Give herself up completely as Paul had wanted? Be someone she couldn't be?

"This isn't a good idea," she said, easing away from his touch and standing.

She hurried to the stairs. She felt him watching her, but she kept going. If she looked back and saw those amazing eyes trailing her every move, she'd give in to her desire to let him take over, and that was something she couldn't do. Ever. No matter how much she wanted to.

"Good job, Baldwin," Luke muttered to himself as he paced the floor in the family room.

Heavy rain from a sudden downpour pelted the roof, cocooning them all tighter in their little nest. Everyone had gone to bed except Derrick, who sat watch outside Dani's door. Luke had also retired for the night, but his conversation with Dani kept playing through his brain like a horror movie. Over and over, he saw her bolt in fear from his touch.

His touch, right! He knew her skin would be as soft as silk, and touching her would just make him want more of her. So why had he given in? It only made her run even farther from him.

A good thing, right? He couldn't commit to anything with her right now, and she was the kind of girl that did serious or not at all. That was one of the reasons he liked her so much.

He pounded a fist onto the desk. The sting to his knuckles and pain radiating up his arm felt good. The computer monitor woke up and live video from the surveillance cameras flashed a view of the house's exterior. He studied the video. All was quiet. Not that he expected Echo to know where they were, but at least it was one less thing for Luke to stew over.

He went to the floor-to-ceiling window and scissored open the blinds to look at the beach. Rough seas pounded against the shore and rain pelted the window. Perfect. Foul and stormy, just like his mood.

He usually enjoyed watching the waves, but his SEAL sense niggled at his brain. Something was wrong. Danger lurked. But where?

He searched through the window. Nothing odd. Just the storm and darkness.

"The storm." Fear surging through his blood, he bolted from the window and up the stairs. He drew his gun and rounded the corner.

Derrick came to his feet. "What is it?"

"The weather on the security feed is perfect, but it's pouring rain outside." Luke stared at Dani's door, the urge to burst in and make sure she was safe sending adrenaline pulsing through him.

Derrick pulled his weapon. "You think Echo hacked the feed and spliced in old footage?"

"Yes." Luke went to Dani's door and pressed his ear against the wood. "Quiet."

"Out of the way, I'm going in," Derrick said, and for the second time today, Luke agreed with the man.

He turned the knob, but the door was locked. He backed up, and with a hard kick, sent the wood splintering and the door flying open.

Dani shot up in bed and grabbed her gun from the nightstand. Relief for her safety made Luke's limbs weak.

She threw off her covers, and her feet were on the floor by the time he entered the room. She was fully dressed, and Luke knew she'd stayed clothed in the event of an attack. He hated that she'd had to plan ahead like this. Couldn't rest. Couldn't find safety no matter where she was.

Derrick charged across the room to the open window.

Drenched curtains slapped against the wall and rain pelted Derrick.

"Did you open the window?" Derrick asked.

"No."

He lowered and locked it. Luke carefully padded across the slippery wood floor and peered out. He spotted a dark figure skulking away.

"There." He pointed to a spot in the distance. "He's there."

"Stay here with Dani. I'm on it." Derrick bolted from the room.

"What's going on?" Dani asked, now fully alert.

Luke turned and caught a shudder traveling over her body.

"You're cold," he said, not wanting to tell her about the video feed. He crossed the room and retrieved her quilt from the bed. He settled the well-worn fabric over her shoulders and tucked it around her neck.

"Please don't ignore my question." She reached up to clasp the corners of the quilt. "Tell me what's going on."

He slipped a finger along her neck and freed a strand of hair caught in the quilt's aged fabric. "Echo hacked into the security feed to cover his tracks while he attempted to break into your room. Thankfully we haven't had rain in a while or footage he chose could've contained rain and we wouldn't have stopped him."

She shivered again, but this time Luke doubted it was from the cold. She was thinking of Echo. As was Luke. Of the man easing the window open while Dani slept not ten feet away. Dressed in black, masked as Dani described him the night of her attack, climbing over the sill. A weapon in his hand, ready to end Dani's life with hollow-point bullets guaranteed to do the job.

Luke should have insisted on someone staying in the room with Dani. He knew he couldn't do that, but Kat or one of her brothers could. And would stay with her now, if Luke had anything to say about it.

Dani closed her eyes for a moment, then flashed them open with a clear sense of purpose shining through. "How did you discover the video feed?"

"I couldn't sleep, so I was wandering around downstairs. I happened to wake up the computer and didn't see any rain falling on what was supposed to be the live feed."

She arched a perfectly plucked brow. "And how did you happen to wake up the computer?"

"Are you wondering if I had something to do with this?"

"No, of course not. It just seems odd that you went anywhere near a computer." She grinned at him, and he wanted to embrace her use of humor over his aversion to computers to lighten the situation, but he couldn't.

Her grin quickly faded. "Is there something else you're not telling me?"

"I slammed my fist into the desk, all right." Embarrassed at his lack of control downstairs, he looked away.

She took his hand, and he felt the quilt fall, then puddle at their feet. He turned back, and at the sight of her slender fingers running over his scraped and bruised knuckles, he drew in a quick breath.

She looked up at him, her eyes wide and alert. "Why did you hit the desk?"

"Because I was frustrated." He took a deep breath and let it out. "I like you, Dani. A lot. There's more than physical attraction between us. But we have too many issues standing in our way. Still, when I touched you and you ran…I…" He let his words fall off and shrugged.

She fixed her gaze on his, sending waves of longing through his body. "You knew it was something special and you thought I didn't."

"Yeah."

"I do, Luke." She gently rubbed her finger over his hand again.

Her touch was driving him crazy, and he could hardly

think straight. He freed his hand, but instead of letting it fall, he threaded his fingers into her hair. Silky and soft, just as he'd imagined.

"But like you said," she continued, "we have too many things standing in our way. Not the least of which is your case. A personal involvement would complicate that."

Would it? Or would it draw them closer together as a team and help them to better track down Echo?

Luke voted for the latter. He was tired of fighting this magnetic pull between them, and he opted for ending the boycott with a kiss. He lowered his head and waited for her to protest, to run from him again, but she gazed up at him expectantly and inched closer. With a groan of surrender, he settled his mouth on lips that had taunted him for days. Soft, sweet, warm, just as he'd known they'd be.

She twined her arms around his neck, drawing him closer, kissing him back. This was right. So right. A spitfire of a woman with a generous heart. Just perfect, and he could keep holding and kissing her and not come up for air.

He vaguely heard a door slam in the distance and felt Dani retreat. She drew in a ragged breath and watched him.

"Luke," she said softly.

He loved hearing his name spoken with such tenderness.

"We can't do this," she whispered.

"Yes, we can."

She took a small step back, regret already burning in her eyes. He reached out a hand to cup her face and keep her near. She let him touch her and closed her eyes.

"What's going on?" a harsh male voice snapped behind him.

Dani jumped and hissed out a breath as he turned to see Kat, Cole and Ethan all standing in the doorway. Kat had a contented look on her face, but the brothers both fired daggers in his direction.

What were they so mad about? He'd just saved their sister

from Echo. But they didn't know that now, did they? As fa
as they were concerned, he was in their sister's bedroom try
ing to kiss her. The brothers were in fact showing far mor
restraint than Luke would have if he found Natalie in a situ
ation like this. He'd act first, then think about it.

He took a step back. "I didn't break down the door to ge
to your sister, if that's what you think. Give me a little mor
credit than that."

"Echo tried to get in." Dani quickly explained the situatio
as her face colored the vivid red of her sweatshirt. "Derric
took off to try to catch him."

"We should wait for Derrick downstairs." Kat grabbed he
brothers' arms as her eyes creased in merriment, not at a
the reaction Luke expected.

"Good idea," Dani said, and bolted for the door nearly a
fast as Derrick had exited earlier.

"Great," Luke mumbled to the empty room. She was run
ning from him again, and he was powerless to stop her. Jus
as he'd been powerless to stop Echo.

He descended to the family room and found Dani seate
at the table, her focus fixed on the security feed on her com
puter. Gun drawn, Cole stood watch at the front door. In th
kitchen, Kat spooned grounds into the coffeemaker.

"You never cease to surprise me, Kit Kat," Cole said a
he shook his head. "I can't believe you can make coffee at
time like this."

"Why not? You're keeping an eye on the door. Dani's mon
itoring the security feed. Ethan's gone after Derrick." Sh
looked up at Luke and a satisfied smile found her lips. "An
with the look on Luke's face right now, I know he wouldn
let anyone get within a hundred feet of Dani. So there's noth
ing for me to do. Plus Derrick and Cole will want somethin
warm when they come inside."

"I want to know how in the world this happened," Dan

mumbled, and rubbed the back of her neck. "I protected the system myself. Echo is good, but he's not better than me."

"Never mind how he hacked it," Luke said as he straddled the chair nearest to Dani. "I want to know how he found the safe house, so when we select another location it'll be secure."

Dani looked up at him. "You've already decided to move me? No discussion."

"It's not safe here," Cole grumbled. "We'll get Ethan to make some calls in the morning to see if we can use one of the bureau's locations. Until then, we need to focus on figuring out how Echo found you."

"Property records would tie the house back to Cole," Luke offered.

Kat set an assortment of handcrafted mugs on the table, then sat in a chair next to Dani. "True, but with the house not being in the Portland metro area, Echo would have had to search every county in the state to find this place."

"Plus he'd have to know about me," Cole added.

"Your name's on the Justice Agency website," Luke said, bringing all eyes his way. "What? I researched your company. Big deal. I'm sure you ran a background check on me."

Kat laughed. "That we did."

Footsteps pounded up the outside stairs. Luke drew his weapon and came to his feet, as did Kat.

Dani tipped her head at the computer. "I can see the front door feed. It's just Derrick and Ethan."

"They could be compromised." Luke returned his focus to the door.

"Ha!" Dani stared at him. "No one else in their right mind would enter this room right now."

Luke glanced at her siblings, both holding weapons, both facing the door. He would find her comment funny if he weren't worried about protecting her. He stepped in front of her, and Kat joined him.

The door opened and Derrick, soaked to the skin, entered

and shook like a dog, spraying water everywhere. Etha
rushed in behind him and secured the door.

"Couldn't catch up to him," Derrick said breathlessly.

A collective sigh came from the siblings. Luke stifled hi
own sigh, as he didn't want the others to know how muc
this situation affected him. Still, as he stepped away fron
Dani, he had to touch her to be sure she really hadn't com
to any harm. He let his fingers brush over her hand. Her eye
flashed wide, and he reveled in the thought that he could tak
her by surprise like this. He thought he'd gotten away with th
brief contact, but when he looked up, Kat gave him a know
ing smile as she returned to the kitchen. She tossed towels t
Cole and Derrick, then grabbed the coffeepot and brought
to the table while the others settled around it.

A flash of the Justice family gathered for special occasion
took his thoughts. As he dropped into a chair at the end c
the table, longing to be part of a large family hit him agair
It was a mistake to think that way. Big mistake. Wouldn'
help him stay away from Dani if he ever called up the nerv
to get close to her again.

"Any progress in figuring out how Echo found us?" Dei
rick rubbed the towel over his head.

"No, but I was about to ask about cell phones," Dani saic
"Did any of you activate GPS on your phones for any reason?

"Are you kidding?" Cole mocked a look of horror. "Afte
your many lectures about people being tracked that way
None of us would dare."

Ethan snorted and Kat clamped down on her lips as i
fighting a laugh. Dani wrinkled her nose at them.

Luke liked how the family could find humor at a time lik
this, but he simply felt unease curdling his dinner. "I don
have a clue if mine is turned on."

Dani held out her hand. "Give me your phone, and I'
check."

He dug out his cell and set it firmly in her open hand. H

fingers brushed her palm and her eyes flared in awareness of his touch, but she quickly veiled it. She tapped the screen, then looked up. "It was on."

"So you led him to us?" Derrick fired a pointed look at Luke.

"Not so fast, Derrick," Dani said as she tapped the phone's screen again. "Echo would have to hack Luke's phone to track the GPS. Unless of course you posted something to Facebook with locations turned on."

"I don't use Facebook." Luke felt horrified that she thought he might.

"No self-respecting SEAL would." Humor lit Cole's tone as he held out his fist to Luke.

Luke pounded his fist and gave a tight smile of appreciation that one of the Justice males seemed to like him.

"Can you tell if his phone's been compromised?" Derrick asked.

When Dani opened her mouth to answer, Ethan quickly held up his hand. "Just a yes or no please. No details."

"Nice," Kat said, mimicking Cole's gesture and fist bumping Ethan.

Dani rolled her eyes. "Yes, but I'll need to spend some time with the phone to be sure."

Luke shook his head. "I didn't even know that was possible."

Dani nodded. "Smartphones are really mini-computers, so it's not only possible, but it happens all the time."

"So how's a guy supposed to protect himself?" He paused and met Dani's gaze. "Or the people he cares about?"

He expected her to look away, but she didn't. "I'll give you lesson on cell phone safety later."

"Great," Luke said sincerely. "I look forward to it."

"I'll just bet you will," Derrick grumbled. "I'm gonna change into dry clothes. I hope you'll have figured out how Echo found us by the time I get back."

Luke hoped the same thing, but he didn't feel confident that they'd easily figure out how a first-class hacker like Echo continued to sidestep their security protocols and threaten Dani's life.

THIRTEEN

Derrick focused a laser-sharp stare on Luke as he filled his mug in SatCom's break room the next morning. It took a lot to make Luke back down, but he felt as if he were wilting under Derrick's focus. He'd trained this same look on Luke last night and kept up this antagonistic attitude since then. Luke could leave the break room and not look back, but he didn't run from anything. And that included the brother of the woman who sent his heart into a dizzying spin despite his common sense.

Luke turned, his coffee sloshing in the cup and lapping close to the edge. "You obviously have a problem with me. I thought once it became clear that I wasn't a traitor you'd lighten up, but if anything it's getting worse."

Derrick leaned against the counter looking deceptively calm. "I don't want Dani to get hurt again."

Neither did Luke, and he harbored fears that if he kept pursuing her when he wasn't free to do so, he could wind up hurting her. But he wasn't going to share that with Derrick. "We're doing everything we can to keep her safe from Echo."

"I don't mean physically. I mean hurt by a guy who's clearly taken with her and will surely break her heart."

Luke arched a brow. Derrick hadn't walked in on the kiss last night, but Luke guessed the other family members had filled him in. Still, how could he know that Luke wasn't ready for a relationship and could hurt Dani?

Derrick crossed his arms. "Pretending you won't hurt her isn't going to make me like you any better."

"Look," Luke said, stepping closer. "I don't care if you like me, but I want you to know it's not my intention to hurt her."

"She tell you about Paul?"

"Yes."

Derrick fisted a hand as if Dani's telling Luke made him mad. "Then you know where she's most vulnerable."

Luke carefully nodded and waited for Derrick to go on. He shoved his hands into his pockets. "See that you don't exploit it."

Luke's chest tightened from having his honor called into question, but he wouldn't back down. "Do you really think I'm that unethical?"

Derrick squinted at Luke, appraising him. "Not on the surface, no. Dani would never fall for a guy who didn't at least portray himself as an honorable guy."

"But you think I'm a snake in the grass like Paul."

Derrick flashed a cold smile. "Could be. Only time will tell."

Luke studied Derrick for a long moment. He was reacting with more emotion than Dani ever had. "I think you have more of a problem over what happened with Paul than Dani has."

"You could be right. But she's my sister, man. No one messes with a guy's sister." His lips pinched in a pained expression.

Luke held up his hands. "Hey, I get it. I have a sister of my own."

"Then if you really are honorable, I can count on you not to treat my sister any differently than you'd want a guy to treat yours."

Despite Derrick's ongoing contempt for Luke, he respected

him for defending his sister. "You're an okay guy, you know that?"

"Don't make me prove otherwise." Derrick turned his back and marched out of the room.

Luke got where Derrick was coming from. He'd do the same thing for Natalie if he felt it needed doing. Problem was, he wasn't the guy he'd just tried to convince Derrick he was. He was the love 'em and leave 'em kind of guy right now. Unless…unless he finally managed to get his father's judgment and condemnation out of his head.

Right, Baldwin. Good luck with that.

He wanted to be optimistic. Wanted to move forward with Dani, but years of trying to rid his brain of his father and failing said it was about as likely to happen as Echo walking through the door and turning himself in.

Dani tried her best to concentrate on Crypton, but she couldn't do it. Echo had hacked Luke's phone, and that bothered her more than many of the other things he'd done. She could handle putting herself in danger, but not someone she cared about.

So that's it, then—you care about Luke. More than you want to admit.

She snorted at her mind's misguided take on Luke.

"What's so funny?" Tim asked from across the table.

"Nothing," she answered quickly.

Tim sat back in his chair and ran his fingers down his goatee. "You seem distracted today."

"I'm sorry. I know how important finishing this review is SatCom's future."

"Yeah, it's that, but I…" He shrugged.

"You what?"

"I'm kinda worried about you." He met her gaze head-on, which was odd for him, and she could see interest burning his eyes.

No, oh, no. Not this.

She'd had her fair share of unwelcome advances over the years and was adept at fending them off, but it usually resulted in hurt feelings. She couldn't add Tim's hurt feelings to everything else that was going on right now. Her best bet was to pretend she didn't see it.

"No need to worry. My family has everything under control." She smiled broadly. "The clock's ticking, so let's get back to work."

His face fell and she quickly looked down at her computer so he wouldn't think she'd seen it.

"Tell me about the change in coding on line 85," she said, though she had no questions about the change.

He launched into his reasoning for making the change and she nodded but kept her eyes glued to the monitor as she processed his feelings.

She'd instantly rejected him because there was no spark between them—at least not on her part—but would dating him be such a bad thing? He shared her interests, and though she'd spent limited time with him, she could tell he was a nice guy. Hardworking. Determined and committed to his job, yet laid-back and considerate. Not bossy like Luke.

Dani flashed a quick look at Luke, who sat behind his desk

If she'd avoided him as she'd just done with Tim, Luke would never have given up. He'd have kept pushing and prodding until she spilled her guts.

She risked a peek at Tim. His head was bent over his keyboard. He was a good-looking guy, in a geeky kind of way. He wore basic T-shirts, jeans and sneakers. A little rumpled but clean and well groomed.

His phone rang, and his head popped up. She quickly looked back at her own computer. Still, she felt his eyes on her as he talked with a staff member about a potential problem.

She heard his chair scrape back and saw him stand. "I've gotta go. I'll be back as soon as I can."

"Problem?" Luke asked.

"Nothing I can't handle in an hour or so." He headed out the door.

Dani felt a sense of relief, and she let out a long breath.

"Hope that's not indicative of how the software review is coming," Luke said.

"What? No, the software is fine. Tim's done a great job so far."

"Any idea of when you might finish the review?"

"Depends on how soon Tim completes the work. What I'm doing right now is preliminary, so when he turns over the final program it'll go quicker."

His brow furrowed. "Can't you sign off on what you've looked at so far?"

She shook her head. "I'll need to receive the final version with no one else having access to change it. Otherwise I can't be sure parts of it haven't been changed after my review."

"Makes sense," he said, though she could tell he wasn't happy about it. His focus shifted to the door.

Holding a cardboard box with Chinese takeout, Kat stepped into the room. The tangy spices quickly saturated the air.

"I ran into Tim in the hallway. He says if we can manage to control ourselves, he'd like us to save a spring roll for him."

"He better hurry back, then." Dani laughed as her stomach rumbled. "I need to wash up."

"Me, too." Kat set the box on the table and winked at Luke. "Leave some for us."

He nodded, but when she expected to see amusement in his eyes she found them narrowed in that pensive gaze that said he was upset about something.

"You okay?" Dani asked.

"Fine."

Dani took a step in his direction. "Is something going on with the case that we need to know about?"

"No." A short answer, but she knew he'd shut down and wouldn't expound on it.

"Okay, then," she said and went into the hall.

"What's with the one-word answers?" Kat asked as she came up beside Dani. "Did you two have an argument or something?"

"Not that I'm aware of. Everything is fine, or so I thought," she replied, but she knew something was wrong.

Maybe it had to do with the kiss last night. Maybe she'd pushed him away one too many times, and if she decided she wanted a chance with him, he wouldn't give her one. Had she blown it, and would she now spend the rest of her life with regrets?

Luke had never been the jealous type, but when Tim had fixed his hungry eyes on Dani a moment ago, Luke had seen red. She didn't seem to return Tim's attention, but a few minutes later, he'd caught her studying him.

Was she considering pursuing Tim? Of course she was. Tim was a stand-up guy. A bit geeky in Luke's opinion, but perfect for Dani. They both liked the same things, and they understood each other, as they'd demonstrated while working together.

"Don't you like the food, Luke?" Kat asked from across the table.

He pulled from his reverie and smiled at her. "It's great."

"So why aren't you eating, then?" She lifted a forkful of rice to her mouth.

"Guess I'm just distracted today."

"You should understand that feeling, Kat." Derrick grinned at Kat, and Luke could see how much he cared about his family. "You've been nothing but distracted since marrying Mitch."

Her grin widened. "Hey, can I help it if I'm happily married? You should try it someday."

"You need to actually be in a relationship before that can happen," Derrick replied sarcastically. "So it's not happening to me any time real soon."

Luke heard a wistful note in Derrick's tone, making the guy seem more human to him.

Great. Just what I need. To forget about Derrick's grumpy attitude and really start liking the guy.

Kat's focus transferred to Luke. "What about you, Luke? Any plans to get married in the future?"

"I'm like Derrick," he said quickly. Maybe too quickly after seeing Dani's face blanch. "I'm really not marriage material right now. With the company in turmoil, I don't have much of an income and couldn't support a wife and family. The way things are going around here, that won't change anytime soon."

Derrick glared at Luke, and he didn't have to ask what it meant. He was warning Luke to stay away from his sister until he got his life together.

"It's good to be settled and all, but I don't agree with waiting for that to happen." Kat picked up her soda and took a sip. "If we wait for the perfect timing most of us would never get married."

Derrick shook his head. "I usually agree with you, Kit Kat. But in this case, Baldwin's right. A guy has to be able to support his family."

Kat set down her soda and focused on her brother. "So if you found the perfect mate and you weren't settled, you'd ignore the feelings? That's like saying God's timing isn't perfect."

Derrick scoffed. "You think God wants us to move forward even when it doesn't make sense?"

"Sometimes." Kat glanced at Dani, then at Luke. "When He's hitting us over the head with a direction He wants us to take and we're ignoring it."

"Hence the perfect-timing comment," Luke mumbled more to himself than to Kat.

"Exactly." She offered him a smile of acceptance. "We usually only think about God's timing when we're waiting for something. You know...we need to be patient and all that. But what about when He's putting something right in front of you and you're refusing to see it? Maybe because you're limiting what you think He can do in your life because you don't think it's possible? But anything's possible for God. Anything." She turned to her sister. "That goes for you, too, sis."

Derrick laughed. "What? Not for me?"

Kat patted her younger brother's arm. "Don't worry. Once you have someone perfect in your life that you're avoiding like Luke and Dani are doing, I'll remind you."

Luke expected him to get angry over his sister's not-so-subtle reference to Dani being perfect for him, but he simply rolled his eyes. "Oh, yeah, we all know how well you like to remind us of things."

Kat laughed and playfully swatted him. Surprisingly Dani didn't argue with Kat's interpretation of things and laughed with them.

Her phone rang. She glanced at the table and her laughter stilled.

"It's Mitch," she said as she answered.

"I'm putting you on speaker, Mitch," she said, forgoing a greeting. "Do you have something on Smash's murder?"

"The ballistics on the gun we recovered after Dani's attack matches the slugs taken from Smash and Grace Evans."

Though Luke was expecting this news, the official confirmation that Echo had killed twice made him draw in a breath.

Dani didn't react at all. "How about prints? Did you lift any from the gun?"

"Yes, but there's no match in the system."

"Basically this doesn't help, then, does it?"

"Not in solving the crime, but it does confirm we're look

ing for the same man who killed your partner. I…" He paused, something Luke had come to know was foreign for the often-blunt guy.

"What is it?" Dani asked.

"Kat would have my hide if I didn't caution you to be careful."

Dani shot a glance at her sister, who chewed on her lip, a sure sign she was worried about this phone call. "I'm here, Mitch. And you're right. I would have your hide." She'd used a light tone, but it fell flat in the room.

Mitch chuckled, but Luke could tell it was forced. "You may think you're invincible, Dani, but we're talking about a serial killer here. Listen to your family for once and let them do what they do best. Protect you."

FOURTEEN

A chair grated against the concrete floor in Luke's office, and he glanced at the table. Dani stood and stretched her arms toward the ceiling as the setting sun cast long shadows into the room. Kat, Derrick and Tim were all still crammed together around the small table. Luke had suggested Derrick and Kat work in the conference room, but after the call from Mitch, neither of them would budge. Obviously the whole family was as stubborn as Dani, and Mitch's comments the other day about becoming part of this family made perfect sense.

"Either we need to be done for the day, or I need a break." Dani dropped her arms to her sides.

Tim looked up at her. "Why don't we call it quits? You've caught up to me, and I'll work faster alone." His gaze ran the length of her body, then back to her face. "Too many distractions with you around."

Luke expected his partner to wink at her, and he felt like throwing up. Instead he crossed the room and got between them so Tim had to take his lecherous eyes off her. Okay, fine, they weren't lecherous, but Luke didn't like another man looking at his Dani that way.

His Dani? Had he decided to move forward and pursue her? To take Kat's advice and trust God's timing? He was clearly throwing them together. So maybe God *did* know what He was doing here.

Was he finally ready to trust that no matter his issues, the timing was right to embrace these feelings for Dani? Could he forget his father's chides and Wendy's hurtful comments and let God take control of his life again?

Am I finally hearing you again, God? Are you telling me to pursue Dani?

Derrick got to his feet and looked out the window. "Since it'll be dark soon and we've never been to the new safe house, it'd be a good idea to take off now."

"Looks like you're out of here, then." Tim closed his laptop and tucked it under his arm. "I'll email you, Dani, if I have any questions."

She nodded and started packing up her computer. Luke breathed a bit easier when Tim left the office. Luke went back to his desk and gathered his work together. When everyone was ready to go, they headed for the door as a group. As Luke clicked off the lights, his printer started spitting out pages, capturing his attention. "That's odd. I didn't send anything to my printer, and it's not connected to the network, so no one else uses it."

"Maybe it's a print job that got caught in the queue and just finished spooling," Dani said.

He turned to her. "In English, please?"

"Something you sent earlier got stuck in line to print and is now printing."

"I haven't printed all day."

"Echo?" Concern darkened her eyes.

Apprehensive over what he might find, Luke flipped the light switch and crossed the room. He heard the Justices step back inside, but they waited by the door as he grabbed the pages from the printer.

He glanced at the first photo. "What in the world?"

He dropped into his chair and quickly flipped through the pictures, each one sending an alarm bell clanging in his head.

"No!" He tossed the papers down, dug out his cell phone and pressed his sister's speed dial.

This can't be happening. Not Natalie.

Dani crossed the room. "What is it? What's wrong?"

He vaguely heard her pick up the discarded pages, but he could think only of Natalie's safety now.

"Nat," he croaked out the moment she answered. "Where are you?"

Dani rattled the stack of papers. "Is this your sister? Is it Natalie?"

Luke couldn't answer. Speaking it aloud made the danger to Natalie's life real, and he'd rather die than think Echo had turned his sights on his only living sister.

Kat and Derrick joined Dani, and she handed the pages to them. Turbulent emotions crossed their faces as they viewed the pictures of a woman going through her day—arriving at work, getting coffee, parking in the lot. Simple tasks that meant nothing on the surface until you realized the person who'd taken these pictures had followed her. Not for an hour, but for a day or longer.

"So you think this is Luke's sister?" Kat asked.

"Seems like it." Dani couldn't take her eyes off Luke.

"It's the man who hacked our network, Nat," Luke said into his phone. "I think he's coming after you."

"Yeah, it's his sister," Dani whispered.

"No! Stay there, Nat. Lock the door and don't let anyone in until I get there."

"That'll take too long." Derrick got in Luke's face, which is what it took to garner his attention. "Let me help you. Where is she?"

"At work. Downtown." Luke turned back to the phone. "I'll be there in twenty minutes, Nat."

"I can have an officer there in less than five," Derrick suggested forcefully.

"She's my sister. I'll take care of it." Luke focused ice-cold eyes on Derrick, reminding Dani that Luke was a rock-solid SEAL who'd been sent on many of the military's most dangerous missions and lived to tell about them.

Derrick didn't back down. "I get that, man, but dispatching an officer to the scene is the safest course of action right now."

They were wasting precious time arguing. Time when Echo could arrive and hurt Natalie. Derrick was thinking clearly and was right about the next move. Dani needed to quickly convince Luke of that.

Hoping a physical touch would snap him out of his state, she stepped between the men and tried to twine her fingers with Luke's. He jerked back as if she'd branded him with fire. Confused, she stood openmouthed.

He grabbed a pen, jotted down an address and thrust the paper at Derrick. "This is where they'll find Natalie. You better not let me down."

Derrick didn't blink but dug out his phone and stepped away. Dani knew he was going to call in a favor at the Portland Police Bureau. He would have an officer on scene just as he'd promised.

"The police are on their way, honey," Luke said to his sister in a soothing tone. "I'll stay on the line until they get there. Then we'll pick you up and take you with us to a safe place." He clamped a hand on the back of his neck and winced. "Don't cry, Nat. Please don't cry."

Dani wanted to comfort him, but clearly he wanted nothing to do with her. That hurt far more than she thought it would. The final days with Paul flashed before her eyes. The sudden change in his behavior. Demanding, pressing, ordering.

She looked at Luke. He was being so soft and sweet to his sister, but for as abrupt as he'd just been to her, he might as well have slammed her against the wall as Paul had done.

Was she wrong about Luke? Had she fallen for a guy who was just like Paul? She was in trouble if she had, because even if he'd just acted harshly, she wanted nothing more than to slide into his arms and comfort him until his sister was rescued.

Luke circled his arm around Natalie and settled back in Derrick's SUV. Dani sat rigidly in the front seat, and despite Luke's happiness at having Natalie safely with him, his heart was heavy. He'd blown it with Dani. He'd hurt her when he'd balked at her help in his office. He hadn't wanted to hurt her. Not for anything in this world and he wished he could take it back.

He would be gentler, kinder, but the result would be the same. They couldn't pursue a relationship. Seeing Natalie in danger told him that letting God take charge of his life again wasn't the right thing to do right now. He needed to take charge as his SEAL training had taught him.

His mission. To protect his sister and Dani at all costs.

And that meant he couldn't be divided in his thinking. Focus was all-important.

See the enemy. Feel the enemy. Destroy the enemy. That's what he had to do.

Derrick pulled up to a boxy home in an older area of Portland. Ethan and Cole stood outside, arms crossed, eyes vigilant. At least Luke had help in taking care of Natalie. Not that he'd let his guard down or let them take charge. She was his to take care of. He had this.

Do you? his mind taunted. *Not without God.*

He'd done just fine without God for the past few years. *Right, look how great you're doing now.*

Cole opened the back door, and Luke pulled his arm free. "Nat, this is Cole Justice."

Natalie gave a tremulous smile much like the ones she'

offered when she'd met Derrick, Dani and Kat. "Nice to meet you."

Cole nodded. "Straight inside."

"I've got it," Luke snapped as he jumped out and instantly regretted it. Cole had been on his side from the beginning. A fellow man in arms. "Sorry, man."

"No worries," Cole said genuinely.

When Natalie climbed out of the car, Luke pressed his hand on her back, urging her up the steps and inside. The home was dark with all the blinds closed tight. They walked through the large dining room leading to a kitchen and then into the adjoining family room in the back of the house.

He encouraged Natalie, whose hands still trembled, to sit. "I'll see if I can find some tea in the kitchen."

"I can make it," Dani offered, her smile reserved for Natalie.

"I don't want to be any trouble," Natalie replied.

"No trouble at all. It'll give me something to do." Dani started searching through grocery bags on the counter, her back stiff.

She clearly didn't want him in the kitchen, so he sat next to Natalie on the sofa. "Try to relax. You're safe here."

She nodded, but her eyes flitted around the room, not lighting on anything. "Why do you think this Echo person came after me?"

He didn't want to add to her anxiety, but he needed to tell her the truth. "He couldn't get to Dani to stop her from working on our software. So he had to find another way to hurt her to make her stop."

"But I didn't even know Dani until today."

"Echo knows Dani's the kind of person who'd be distraught if anyone, even a perfect stranger, got hurt because of her." He glanced at Dani and wished with all he had that he could go back an hour and have a redo.

"You care for her," Natalie said softly.

He didn't answer but continued to watch Dani. Her movements were smooth and effortless, her concentration intense. Even when making a cup of tea, she gave it her all. Even when she'd fought her attraction to him, she'd still been there when he'd talked about losing his family. About his father's problems. And he'd given her nothing. So what difference did it make that he cared about her? She needed someone who was free to return her feelings.

"Luke?" Natalie asked.

"She's a very special person," he answered, not wanting to admit he'd fallen for her and blown his chances.

"But you're not going to do anything about it, are you?"

"No."

Natalie took his hands. "Don't let Wendy's attitude ruin your life."

"I'm not. I'm just being practical." He forced out a smile. "Let me find some paper and you can make a list of things you want from home."

She arched a brow.

"What?"

"You're changing the subject."

He gave her a wistful smile as he rose. "Hang tight. I'll be right back."

He went into the kitchen and opened drawers.

"Can I help you with something?" Dani asked, sounding like a perfect stranger.

How about not looking at me like I'm a slug crawling out from under a rock?

"I need something to write on." Barely able to keep it together under her watchful eyes, he looked away.

"I have a notepad in my bag," she said dispassionately, as if she didn't care what became of him at all.

She dug out the pad as the teakettle whistled its readiness.

"Thanks for looking after Natalie," he said, hoping to start a meaningful conversation.

"It's the least I can do. She doesn't deserve any of this." Dani turned her back and went to the stove.

Utterly deflated, he took the notepad to Natalie as the Justice clan filed into the room. A grim look of determination marked their faces, and Luke wondered if something else had happened. But he wasn't going to ask about it in front of Natalie and upset her more.

"Gather around." Ethan gestured for them to join him in the family room.

Luke waited to see where everyone landed before deciding what to do. Dani entered the room with trepidation and handed the mug to Natalie, then took a seat in an overstuffed chair. Kat joined Natalie on the sofa. Derrick perched on the arm of Dani's chair as if he were staking his claim. Cole and Ethan sat in chairs facing the sofa. Still not knowing where to sit, Luke leaned against the fireplace.

"We need to form a watch schedule." Ethan braced one leg on the other. "I want two people to stand duty whenever Dani and Natalie are here. I've already cleared Cole's and my schedule so we can cover the house when no one else can."

"Natalie will be here 24/7." Luke fired a this-is-not-optional look at his sister.

"I can't take off work," Natalie protested.

Luke intensified his look. "There's nothing too important in your schedule that's worth risking your life over. You'll stay here."

She nodded.

A chunk of Luke's apprehension disappeared with her agreement. "You don't have to schedule me. I'll be right here all night, every night until this is resolved."

"No need. I'll already be here." Derrick sat up straight as if he thought it would make Luke back down.

Luke pushed off the mantel and pulled his shoulders back. "Then I guess we'll be spending a lot of time together."

Derrick crossed his arms. "I guess we will."

"Let's move on." Kat dramatically wiped the back of her hand across her forehead. "I'm dying from all the testosterone flowing through the room."

Despite the tension, the family members laughed. All except Dani, who was watching him like she might watch a computer virus invade one of her precious machines. A virus she intended to eradicate.

He'd come on too strong with Natalie again. Dani already thought he was too controlling, and this blatant display of bossiness reinforced her take on him. One of these times he needed to think before speaking. But, come on. Her life was on the line. He never let those he cared about face danger without his protection, and he might as well admit it, he cared about her. Too much. So whether she liked it or not he'd be on duty all night. There was no way he was letting Echo get the jump on them again.

FIFTEEN

Dani finished stacking the last of the dinner dishes in the dishwasher and looked up. Luke had planted himself in the adjoining family room, his head down, looking at his phone. Dinner had been an awkward event thanks to the tension flowing between her and Luke. Natalie, on the other hand, had taken Luke's demands in stride and had relaxed. Dani took that to mean Natalie was not only used to the caveman treatment from her brother, but she accepted it.

Kat pulled the plug in the sink and the water gurgled down the drain. "We should get the room arrangements settled."

Dani wanted to help Kat, but she wasn't sure if it was a good idea to leave her brothers alone with Luke. No telling what they might decide on her behalf.

Kat tugged on Dani's arm, dragging her into the family room and not giving her a chance to say no. "We're going to choose rooms, Natalie. Do you want to join us?"

"Sure," she said, and came to her feet.

Dani couldn't get over how much Natalie resembled Luke. Her features were much finer than his and she had a cute little nose, but both had dark hair and ice-blue eyes.

Kat started for the stairs, then turned back. "You guys have any preferences?"

Cole and Ethan, who sat at a small table playing checkers, shook their heads.

"I won't be needing a room," Luke said.

"Me, neither." Derrick bumped out his chest as if he were trying to one-up Luke.

Dani chose to ignore her brother and Luke's sparring. "If anything comes up while I'm gone, please wait for me to come back. I want to be involved in any decisions."

"Don't worry." Cole smiled at her. "We got your message loud and clear. I'll make sure you're consulted."

"Thanks." Dani returned Cole's smile with an earnest one. She loved how much happier he'd been since Alyssa and her children had come into his life.

Dani joined Natalie and Kat, who'd made it to the second-story landing. They pulled suitcases brought in by Cole and Luke after he'd gone to his house to retrieve Natalie's things. Seeing Natalie's limp made Dani think of the fire. How horrible it must have been to survive such an ordeal only to discover her mother and sister perished. How horrible for Luke to feel guilty for not being there. She couldn't begin to put herself in his place. He had a right to be so protective of his sister, and she completely understood why he'd reacted as he had when he'd received the pictures of Natalie.

Did Dani's family have the same right? Had she been too hard on them?

"Coming, Dani?" Kat called over her shoulder.

Dani shook off her thoughts and would bring them out again when she was alone. "On my way."

She followed the sound of wheels humming over the wood floor. The noise suddenly stopped as Kat and Natalie paused to peek into the first bedroom. Dani joined them, noting the room held two twin beds.

"This will be our room, Dani," Kat said. "There aren' enough bedrooms for everyone, so we can share."

Normally Dani didn't mind sharing with her only sister but tonight she wanted privacy so she could ponder the sit uation with Luke and seek God's guidance. "The guys can bunk together."

Kat narrowed her eyes. "I know they can, but I won't let you spend the night alone."

"So you don't think I can take care of myself, either?"

"Echo has proven his prowess in finding us. I won't let him hurt you." Kat jutted out her chin.

Dani crossed her arms. Kat raised her shoulders higher. They stared at each other as they had during disagreements growing up. The first to blink usually lost. Kat's lip poked out and her determination flowed from her face. Dani doubled her effort.

Natalie stepped between them. "You two are so cute together. Pretending to be so tough when you both want the same thing."

Was she serious?

Dani eyed Natalie to gauge her sincerity.

She laughed. "I'm the youngest in the family, too, Dani. I know you get pushed around a lot, but life is fragile. You could lose each other in the blink of an eye. Take the time to appreciate each other, too. I'd give anything to have a chance to see my sister and my mom again."

Convinced she'd behaved small and petty, Dani stepped closer to Natalie. "Luke told me about the fire. I'm so sorry for your loss."

Natalie's mouth fell open. "Luke told you?"

Dani nodded. "Is that a problem?"

Natalie waved her hand in the air. "No, no. It's just…he's never shared it with anyone else."

Despite Dani's displeasure with Luke's heavy-handed behavior, her heart warmed. The big, tough guy had opened up to her, and she hadn't realized how important that was. But Natalie obviously did as she scrutinized Dani.

Dani felt a blush rise up her neck to her cheeks. She was not going to let Natalie see how much her brother affected her.

"Let's find a room for you," she said, and took off down the hall.

Dani heard them following, but she didn't turn until after they'd selected a room for Natalie.

"We'll leave you to get settled." Dani started to walk away.

"Wait," Natalie called out. "Would you mind hanging out with me for a bit? I'm still freaked out about everything that's going on."

"I'll put your stuff in our room." Kat grabbed the handle of Dani's suitcase and headed down the hall.

Not sure if spending time alone with Luke's sister was a good idea, Dani didn't answer immediately.

Natalie looked uneasy. "I understand if you don't want to stay."

"No, it's fine. I'm glad to keep you company."

Natalie didn't waste a moment but pulled her suitcase into the room and placed it on the bed. Dani sat in a small chair in the corner.

Natalie pulled the zipper on her suitcase and narrowed those cobalt-blue eyes exactly like Luke's. "This is really surreal, isn't it? Or are you used to this kind of thing?"

Dani shrugged. "I'm used to providing protection for clients, but being the official object of protection is new to me."

"Official?" Natalie lifted a toiletry bag from the suitcase. "I don't understand."

"Like you said, as the youngest, I'm used to everyone bossing me around. But I've never been whisked away to a safe house where they train their professional skills on me. It's kind of daunting. Now I understand how our clients must feel."

Natalie perched on the edge of the bed. "Being the baby of the family can be tough."

"But you didn't seem to mind giving in when Luke said you couldn't go to work."

Natalie took her pajamas from the suitcase. "It used to

bother me. Quite a bit actually. Until Hannah and Mom died. Luke blames himself for their deaths. So he's overly protective of me. If taking responsibility for my safety helps him get through the day, I'm fine with that."

Dani recalled the pain in Luke's eyes when he'd told her about the fire. He carried such a heavy burden, and she'd done nothing to help him with it. In fact, she'd made it worse for him by balking every time he tried to help her. "He shouldn't blame himself."

"We both know that, but he's got to work through this for himself." Natalie smiled. "Until then, I'll support him however I can."

"You're a good sister," Dani said.

"So are you."

Dani thought about how much she fought her brothers. The grief she gave them, especially Derrick, when they were simply showing that they cared for her by watching out for her. "I'm not so sure about that."

"I can see that you have a good heart even when they're pushing your buttons."

"If you say so," Dani said. "But I'm going to try to respond more like you from now on."

"Maybe it's easier for me."

"Why's that?"

"After living with our dad, I feel like Luke's bossiness is minor." Her eyes took on a faraway look. "Dad was a drill sergeant like no other. Everything had to be his way down to the littlest thing. He didn't do it out of love like Luke does. He was just a big bully."

"I'm sorry, Natalie."

She shrugged. "We all have our past issues to deal with. But you see, this is how I know Luke is a good guy. He's nothing like our dad. He's warm and caring. Gentle, even." Natalie locked gazes with Dani. "And he's a real catch, so you should get over whatever's keeping you from following your feelings."

Dani's mouth dropped open.

Natalie giggled. "Yeah, I can see you both care for each other."

Dani didn't know what to say.

Natalie patted her knee. "I'm only telling you this because he hasn't shown an interest in a woman since his fiancée broke up with him. She left him feeling like he needed to have a steady income before he could ever hope to marry, so I want to encourage his interest."

Dani wished she could say she wanted to encourage Luke, too, but after this conversation, she really didn't know what she wanted.

I'm so confused, Father. What do You want me to do here?

Natalie suddenly sat back. "I've put my foot in it, haven't I?"

"What? No. It's fine. I'm just a little confused about the whole thing right now and could really use some time to think."

"Then you should go."

"You'll be okay alone?"

"Yes." Natalie wrinkled her round little nose. "I wasn't completely honest before. I really wanted to talk to you about Luke in private. I hope you're not mad."

Dani didn't need Natalie inserting herself in her private life, as she had plenty of brothers and sisters who already felt free to do so, but the conversation had given her insight into Luke's behavior so it had been worth it.

"I'm not mad at all." Dani smiled at Natalie, then slipped out of the room. She ran into Kat in the hallway.

"Everything okay with Natalie?" Kat asked.

"Yeah. She wasn't freaked out, but wanted to talk about Luke."

"Ah, she sees it, too, huh?" Kat leaned against the wall. "You and Luke, I mean."

Dani nodded.

"And you still can't let go of what happened with Paul to embrace your feelings?"

"I know he's not like Paul, but he still has this obsessive need to protect the women in his life." Dani shook her head. "You of all people should understand I can't live like that."

"So what you're saying is, you'd prefer a man who ignored the fact that your life was in danger and let you do whatever you felt like doing?"

"I didn't say that."

"Yes, you did. You can't have it both ways, Dani. You can't want a man to be strong and protective yet laid-back and meek."

"I just want a man who's supportive of my career and of the independence I've tried so hard to find."

"Other than the danger present, has Luke ever done or said anything to make you think he doesn't like independent women?"

"No."

"Does his sister think he's controlling other than wanting her to stay safe?"

"No."

"Then open your eyes, girl. See the whole man. Not just the part that you want to see so you don't have to risk getting hurt again."

Kat was right. It was time for Dani to let go of any notion that Luke was like Paul. To recall the way he treated Natalie. He'd clearly do anything for her. His career record showed he was honorable. And despite her constant rebuff of him, he'd remained compassionate. Plus she'd never forget the intense ache he'd displayed over losing his family.

"You look like you're in shock," Kat said.

"A few things are finally starting to sink in."

Kat grabbed Dani and gave her a bear hug.

"Ouch," Dani said. "You don't have to squeeze the life out of me."

Kat leaned back. "I'm just so happy that you've found someone."

Dani laughed. "What is it with you people in love? You go all gushy."

Kat smiled widely. "In this case, gushy is a good thing, sis. Trust me on this and don't let Luke get away."

"I'll try."

"Speaking of gushy, I need to call Mitch and say goodnight." With a sappy grin on her face, Kat hurried down the hallway and Dani raised her face.

I'm sorry, Father, for not trusting You with this problem. I know I've dishonored You by trying to rely solely on myself. Help me to see the Luke You want me to see and to act accordingly.

The tension in her body relaxed and she felt hopeful. She'd moved forward. Made a decision. Now all she had to do was remember her prayer when she saw Luke again and maybe, just maybe, she could let go and respond to the feelings that she'd been avoiding for days.

SIXTEEN

Feeling like he might jump out of his own skin, Luke strode back and forth at the base of the stairs leading to the bedrooms. He wasn't used to feeling this way. He was well trained. Calm in the face of danger. But he didn't understand or have any skills in the kind of danger Echo brought.

So that meant he felt a need to be physically next to Dani every moment, and that wasn't an option right now. She had to sleep. Though he would gladly sleep on the floor by her bed, the Justice men would never allow such a thing. He had to settle for Kat sleeping in the bed next to her.

He'd expected Derrick would camp outside her door, but he sat at the dining table, his computer next to him where he could monitor security cameras. Ten cameras surrounded the home, and no one, not even someone as skilled as Luke, would have an easy time of breaching this house unseen. But then Luke didn't possess the ability to disable security systems. Echo did.

Luke continued to pace. He could feel Derrick's gaze following him. Back and forth. Back and forth.

"C'mon, man," Derrick said. "Sit down, for crying out loud. You're making me nervous."

Luke took a seat across the table from Derrick. He looked at the youngest Justice male. Looked at a face that was too reminiscent of Dani to let him sit still. He bounced his knee.

"You always this jumpy?" Derrick picked up a deck of cards and shuffled.

The rippling of the cards irritated every nerve ending in Luke's body. His SEAL sense was telling him not to relax. Not for a moment, but he'd burn out if he kept up this level of intensity. Burning out would do no good if he had to act quickly.

"Everything okay on the monitors?" he asked, and rolled his neck.

"Fine."

"And you're sure the system hasn't been hacked?"

"Yes." Derrick started laying out the cards for a game of solitaire. "If it helps, she feels the same way."

"What?"

"Dani. She returns your feelings."

He thinks this is about how I feel? "So now you're going to warn me off again?"

"Nah."

Luke's head popped up and Derrick laughed. "I've been watching you, and I'm starting to think you're the real deal."

"In other words, even your deep background check didn't return anything."

"Something like that." Derrick laughed again and Luke felt himself relax a notch.

Derrick held up the cards. "Want to play something to kill the time?"

Luke had spent many hours playing cards in his military career, so he nodded. "Better prepare yourself to get skunked, though."

Derrick's eyebrow went up. "As if."

Luke laughed and settled into his chair. Maybe tonight would pass without a hitch. Maybe, but he knew better. Whenever he'd started to think like that on a mission, his world collapsed around him and someone usually paid with their life.

* * *

Dani couldn't sleep. Now that she'd decided to lower the wall she'd erected between her and Luke, she kept remembering his touch. His kiss. His tenderness and kindness. None of which made it easy to fall asleep.

She swung her legs out of bed and shivered in the nippy air. Grabbing a sweatshirt, she pulled it on and slipped her feet into athletic shoes. To keep from waking Kat, she crept to the door and padded toward the stairs. She paused at the landing to look down on the family room. Luke and Derrick sat across from each other at the dining table. They snapped cards onto the glass and an occasional laugh broke out.

Derrick wouldn't laugh with Luke unless he'd decided Luke was okay. Seemed like all the Justices had now decided Luke was a good guy. It took a lot to fool her entire family, especially Kat, whose radar went up whenever she perceived a family member was about to get hurt. She'd stopped questioning whether Luke was a good guy days ago.

And now Dani had done the same thing. Question was, what did she do about it? Luke had made it clear that he wasn't ready for a relationship unless SatCom succeeded. She could aid in that by finishing her review of Crypton on a timely basis so the committee could consider it. She'd spend the night reviewing the software again so tomorrow she could simply compare the programs, evaluate any changes and finish her review before the day ended.

She headed down the stairs to get her laptop. Both men were so intent on their game that they didn't notice her heading their way.

Suddenly Luke jumped to his feet, grabbed his weapon and spun in one fluid movement that rivaled a choreographed dance. Feet planted wide, nostrils flared, he aimed his gun at her heart, and she jumped back at the intensity in his eyes. An intensity that mimicked Paul's when he'd finally snapped.

Air whooshed from his lungs, and his arms fell limply to the side. "Man, Dani. With this family, I'd think you'd know better than to sneak up on a guy."

"I wasn't sneaking," she said defensively. Paul had made her feel like the bad guy, too. Blaming her for the way he felt.

Luke slammed his gun into the holster and grabbed the house keys from the table. "I'm going to check the perimeter." He marched out the front door, pulling it firmly closed and locking it behind him.

"Nice one," Derrick said as she sat next to him. "I just got him to relax a bit and you put him right back into hyper SEAL mode."

"I didn't do anything but walk into the room."

"And maybe fall for the guy."

She arched a brow.

"Don't bother to deny it. You know you can't hide anything from me."

"I don't need to try now that you seem more reasonable about Luke."

"Are you going to do anything about it?"

She shrugged. "I think about it and then he goes all stalker on me like he just did, and I want to run screaming."

"That wasn't stalker mode. His reaction was simply instinct honed in years of intensive training to become a SEAL. Derrick got up. "Don't confuse the two or you might miss out on something good like I did."

Dani figured he meant Gina Evans, the woman he'd been serious about in college until she'd bailed on him their senior year. Dani hadn't realized that Gina had left such a deep scar, but then all the Justices were very good at hiding their feelings. From each other and from anyone who threatened to break through walls they'd erected to protect hearts still tender from the loss of their parents. Even though she now knew she wanted to knock down her wall, would she be able to?

* * *

Late the next day Dani approached Luke's desk and laid her official report recommending Crypton in front of him. "Crypton is ready for the committee."

Luke jumped to his feet. "We're good. For real?"

"For real."

"Thank you." Laughing, he grabbed her in a bear hug and swung her around. She felt light as a feather as she reveled in his excitement. The two of them were alone for the time being, and she couldn't be happier that she could share this moment with him without others watching.

He set her down and looked into her eyes. "If the committee contracts with us I owe it all to you."

She didn't want to burst his bubble, but she knew he still had a steep hill to climb before the committee accepted the work. "Why don't you call Wilder and see if you can get on his schedule?"

"Good idea, but first…" He planted a kiss on her cheek and peered at her. "Thank you for believing in me. For helping me get closer to achieving my dream. Even when I've been a jerk like yesterday." He paused and ran a hand over his head. "I'm sorry about how I behaved. You didn't deserve that."

"Don't worry about it. I understand."

His eyes filled with hope. "You do, honestly?"

She nodded.

"If we secure this contract, I…" His words trailed off and he shook his head. "We'll wait to talk when and if that happens."

"Sounds good," she said, hoping by the time they had their talk she would trust him enough to let down her wall.

He dialed the general and she waited to hear the verdict. When he'd hung up, he held up his soda can for a toast. "He's agreed to see me. Thanks to you."

She clunked her can against his and let a wave of happiness wash over her.

"You two look happy," Kat said from the doorway, then went to the table to jot something on a notepad before ripping off the page.

Luke shrugged into his jacket. "Dani finished her review, and I'm on my way to meet with General Wilder."

"Excellent news." Kat clapped her hands and turned to Dani. "Does this mean we can head out for the day?"

"Why so eager to get going?"

"Mitch said he can get off a little early today and meet me at the safe house."

"As much as I'd like to stay and talk about mushy stuff like your marriage to Mitch, I need to get going." Luke chuckled as he put the report in his portfolio.

"Good luck," Dani said.

He settled the portfolio under his arm and stepped to her. He tucked a stray strand of hair behind her ear, then cupped the side of her face.

"Thank you again." His face lit with a breathtaking smile. "I'll call you as soon as I know anything."

Nearly forgetting to breathe, she nodded and watched him rush out of the room.

"Wow," Kat said. "The temperature in here went up twenty degrees with that look."

Dani swatted at her sister, then threw her arm around her. "Let's get out of here so you and Mitch can do a little temperature-raising of your own."

"I've located the owner of Computer Care's building." Kat handed the page she'd torn from the notepad to Dani. "Name look familiar?"

Dani looked at the paper. Anthony Jackson. Not someone she knew. She tucked the page into her pocket. "I'm assuming you were able to locate this guy."

Kat nodded. "His secretary is trying to fit in a meeting with us as soon as possible, and she'll call me back."

As Derrick went to get the car, they packed up and th

three of them were soon fighting rush-hour traffic. Dani sat next to Derrick in the front and Kat rode in the back. Despite the horns honking and cars congesting the roads, Dani's mind kept drifting from life around her to Luke's appointment with General Wilder. Luke desperately wanted his company to succeed, and she wanted the same thing for him. Maybe as desperately as he did.

Let this happen, Father. For Luke. He deserves this. Please.

Kat's phone rang. "It's the owner of Computer Care's building."

Dani swiveled in time to see Kat answer, then give her full attention to the call. Feeling like everything was falling into place, Dani hoped he'd provide the lead they needed to locate Echo and bring him to justice.

"Can you hold on for a moment?" Kat cupped her hand over the phone. "His assistant says he's leaving town in a couple hours. He'll see us for a few minutes or we'll have to wait until he gets back in two weeks."

"Waiting isn't optional." Dani faced Derrick. "We could go over there right now."

Derrick glanced in his rearview mirror, likely getting Kat's take on the risk this stop might entail.

"I'm good with it," she said.

He gave a clipped nod. "Looks like we're making a detour."

Dani clutched his arm and smiled her thanks as Kat got directions from the assistant. She hung up and shared the address with Derrick. Dani glanced at her watch. With rush hour and the owner's address located on the far side of downtown, they'd likely arrive at the safe house later than Luke. He'd worry if she wasn't there when he arrived.

"I'll call Cole and tell him about our delayed ETA so he doesn't worry," Kat said as if she was reading Dani's mind.

"I'll send Luke a text, too." Dani pulled out her phone. "With the tight security at the naval facility he won't have his phone in the meeting, but at least when he gets out he'll know where we are."

Traffic slowed to a standstill and Derrick looked at her, his face awash with humor. "Checking in with hubby already."

She rolled her eyes and typed the text, then settled her phone in her lap and sat back for the long drive.

A few minutes later, her phone chimed and, hoping it was Luke with an update on his meeting, she grabbed it. When she spotted Tim's name, her heart fell. Still, she gave him a cheerful hello.

"I'm glad I caught you," he said. "We've had another breach of the network."

"He's tenacious, I'll give him that."

"Tenacious, yes, but foolish. I was able to track the transmission to a local address."

"You did?" Dani said, surprised that Echo would be so careless, and suddenly she suspected he was setting a trap to lure her out into the open.

Tim laughed. "Don't sound so surprised. I'm as good as you are, you know."

"I know," she responded and meant it. She'd seen his work firsthand the past few days and knew he possessed top-notch skills. "Give me the address. Maybe we can stop by after our meeting."

"You mean you don't want to go straight there?"

Not if it's a trap. "I really need to meet with the building owner first."

"But the hacker could take off."

"We'll just have to risk it." She hoped she wasn't wrong here, but her gut said their appointment with Computer Care's building owner was more important.

Tim rattled off the address and Dani punched it into the car's GPS so she wouldn't forget it. "I'll let you know if we find anything."

"So you're still going to your meeting first?" he asked one more time.

"Yes. I'll let you know how it goes." She said goodbye before he tried to argue further.

She turned to Derrick. "That was Tim. The network's been hacked again. He tracked the transmission to a local address."

"Let me guess. You want to go over there."

"Maybe after the meeting."

He arched a brow. "It's not like you to wait."

"My gut says it's a trap. Like when Computer Care exploded. It would be better to make a plan before going in."

Kat sat forward. "I don't want you going anywhere near that address. We'll drop you at the safe house and then we'll check it out."

Dani knew they were right. She'd do the same thing with someone under her care. Still, she crossed her arms in frustration and stared out the window.

"Don't pout," Derrick said.

"I'm not pouting."

"Yes, you are, Twinkie."

She rolled her eyes at him again and returned to looking out the window. The car was barely inching forward. "We should have taken side streets instead at this time of day."

"When you're driving, you choose the route. When I'm driving—" His words fell off as he leaned on the horn at a car cutting them off. He fell silent and Dani was thankful for the quiet to prepare her mind for the meeting.

Thirty minutes later, they exited into downtown Portland and laboriously made their way through the city clogged with traffic. Finally they turned onto a deserted side street and Dani's hope that they'd arrive in time to meet with the owner rose.

Derrick must have sensed her urgency and sped up. As they passed an alley, a black SUV came out of nowhere and barreled toward them.

"Look out," Dani screamed. She tried to scoot closer to Derrick, but before she could move, the SUV slammed into the rear door on her side.

The sickening sound of metal grinding on metal split the air. Dani's side airbag exploded. Her head snapped to the side and the rough fabric burned along her cheek.

She clawed at the airbag as the SUV shoved them onto the sidewalk, and she caught a quick glimpse of the driver. He wore a black ski mask, the same as the night she'd been attacked.

Echo?

He gunned the vehicle, and the SUV's engine roared in her ears. The powerful car's tires spun, then caught, ramming their car into the building.

Another airbag exploded, and she heard Derrick groan. Their car rocked back and forth, making her feel like a rag doll. When it settled, she faced Derrick. He was alive and moving. She turned to Kat, who lay on the floor, blood on her head. She wasn't moving.

"Kat." Dani swiveled.

"Kat," Derrick repeated as he looked into the mirror.

"She's not moving," Dani screamed, panic taking her voice high.

She struggled to unbuckle her seat belt to check on Kat, and Dani saw Derrick's face pale. She searched him for injury and found blood saturating his pant leg.

"I'm pinned." He took deep breaths and let them out slowly.

"We need to stop your bleeding first, then I'll check on Kat." Agony bit into Dani. This was all her fault. Her family was suffering because of her.

Shaking hands made slow work of unbuckling her seat belt. Finally free, she got to her knees. Her door was jerked open behind her. Dani didn't turn to look, but saw Derrick reach for his gun. Before he drew, an arm slid around her waist and the cool end of a gun barrel bit into her temple.

"Don't think about it," the distorted male voice said. "Dani and I are taking a little trip and you're staying right here. Come after her and she dies."

Dani recognized the voice and the man's scent as the same man who'd attacked her in her home. Echo!

He started to drag her backward, and she struggled against his iron-tight arms. "Derrick will bleed out. I need to stop the bleeding."

Derrick met her gaze. "Stop fighting, Dani."

"No," she whispered, but she knew he was right. Echo wouldn't let her help either of her siblings. He'd simply kill her or both of them. Tears threatened and she blinked hard to fight them.

Echo kept his arm around her but set a plastic grocery bag on the seat. "Gather everyone's phones."

"No, please. At least let them call for an ambulance."

He ground the barrel into her skin. "Get the phones. Now."

Wincing in pain, Derrick dug his phone out of his pocket and dropped it into the bag. Dani leaned over the backseat and Echo moved with her. She found Kat's phone on the floor.

"Kat," she whispered. "I love you, sweetie. Please be okay."

"Wasn't that sweet." Echo jerked her backward.

"I love you, Derrick," she cried out as Echo hauled her out the door and toward his vehicle.

"You, too, Twinkie." The sadness in Derrick's voice opened the dam and tears dripped down her cheek.

Father, please, she begged. *Get help here as soon as possible. I can't lose either one of them.*

SEVENTEEN

General Wilder met Luke at his office door. His usual no-nonsense expression was replaced by sympathy. Not good. Wilder rarely wore emotions on his sleeve, and his expression told Luke all he needed to know. SatCom was finished.

"I'm sorry for bringing you all the way over here," Wilder said, not even offering for Luke to take a seat. "I just met with committee members and they voted to extend a contract to Security-Watchdog tomorrow."

Luke's stomach tied in a gut-wrenching knot.

He'd lost.

His dream was over.

He waited for the feeling of failure to settle in. To hear his father's voice again, but it didn't come.

No guilt. Not a bit. Sure, hurting his staff and failing in his promise to Hawk stung, but his only emotion now was sadness. Deep, fatiguing sadness.

In one sweep of the committee's strong arm, thoughts of a relationship with Dani evaporated. Poof. Right before his eyes. Gone. He cared so much about her. Deeply and helplessly, and he wanted to be with her, but he'd wait to pursue her until he found himself on solid ground.

"Baldwin," Wilder said.

Luke shook off his melancholy and pulled back his shou

ders to bid the general goodbye. "I appreciate all the chances you've given SatCom. And for the many times you've gone to bat for us."

"I wish we could have parted under better circumstances." Wilder clapped Luke on the back and shook his hand with an iron grip. "I'm sure there will be future contracts for you to bid on."

"Of course," Luke replied, though he was sure SatCom was done for. "Take care."

On the way out of the U.S. Naval and Marine Corps Reserve facility, Luke grabbed his cell phone from security. He noted the text light blinking, but he was in no mood to deal with it, so he shoved the phone into his pocket. He'd check the text once he got to his car, where he could lick his wounds in private.

He strode across the lot, nearly running to get away from the awful truth of losing the contract. The sun shone brightly on him. The warmth usually improved his mood, but he didn't care.

Kat's words flashed into his brain. *God's timing is perfect.*

Was it? Was he supposed to ignore the failure of his company, not to mention his penniless status, and tell Dani how he felt? God certainly didn't want that for Dani, did He?

"No way," Luke mumbled, and slid into his car.

He sat there, hands on the wheel, wondering what to do next. His phone beeped, reminding him of the text, so he dug it out. At the sight of two messages from Dani, his heart crumbled over his situation. He pressed the icon.

Meeting with Computer Care's building owner on the way to the safe house. He has the name and location of Computer Care's owner. Will keep you updated. Hope the meeting went well with Wilder.

Good. They had a lead. He moved to the second message.

Network was hacked again today. Tim traced it to a local address. Heading over there after our meeting. Call me when you're free.

His company and Dani might be lost to him, but they might still be able to put the person responsible for the sabotage behind bars. Hoping for good news, he dialed Dani's number. The phone rang five times and went to voice mail. In case she was still in a meeting, he sent her a text and waited for a reply. Time ticked by. No response. He dialed Kat. Same response. Five rings and straight to voice mail. Worry cut a path through his heart, and that niggle of warning he'd developed as a SEAL burrowed into his brain. If Dani was in trouble, Natalie might be, too.

He didn't have Derrick's number or he'd be dialing him already. He did have the restricted number for the safe house. He could check on Natalie and Cole, or Ethan could give him Derrick's number. He made the call.

"Cole Justice," he answered warily.

"It's Luke. Is Natalie okay?"

"Fine. Why?"

Luke sighed a quick breath of relief over his sister, but worry for Dani kept his stomach in a knot. "Dani and Kat were on the way to meet with the building owner for Computer Care and they aren't answering their cells. My gut says something's wrong. I don't have Derrick's number. Either give it to me or call him."

"Hold on," Cole said patiently, though Luke had been testy. "I'll call him on my cell."

Luke heard Cole moving in the background. A few short moments later, he came back on the phone. "No answer with Derrick. I sent all of them a 911 text. One of them is bound to respond."

Luke waited, but as each second ticked by, his gut tightened more.

"No response," Cole said.

"Something's definitely wrong." Luke started his car as his mind flew over what to do.

"I concur. We need to find them."

"Dani's files should hold the building owner's name. I'll call Tim to look at them and get back to you."

Luke disconnected and dialed his partner. No answer. Not unusual for Tim. He preferred to communicate through text. Luke wasn't going to mess around with Tim not responding. He sent a 911 text. As he waited, he pointed his car out of the lot so he was ready to move.

Tim hadn't responded by the time Luke reached the road to the security gate. Luke slammed a fist on the wheel.

Where was everyone?

He glanced at his watch. His assistant would be gone for the day. Luke had no choice but to head back to the office to look. He was at a minimum thirty minutes away from the office, but depending on traffic, it could take nearer to an hour.

"Too long," he mumbled, and pressed Dani's icon on his phone again. Only three rings this time and no answer.

Luke wound through traffic and merged onto I-5. When he saw the brake lights ahead, he knew his only hope of getting to the office on a timely basis was to give up on his self-reliance and ask for God's help to get him through the traffic. And while he was at it, he needed to put Dani in God's hands and know He would care for her. Something Luke had little experience doing of late.

Echo forced Dani into a metal chair in an old abandoned warehouse. Holding his gun against the back of her head, he twined thick ropes around her body and tightly lashed her to the chair.

Fear climbed up her throat and threatened to choke her. How would anyone find her here?

The address Tim had given her was in this area of town. Made sense that Echo would take her to a place he frequented. Hopefully Kat and Derrick were all right and they'd think to look at the address she entered in the GPS, then send someone to rescue her. Her heart constricted at the thought of leaving them behind. She'd alternated praying for her siblings on the drive here with asking this creep to let her go. Echo hadn't spoken a word since he'd dragged her away from Derrick. He'd simply held his gun to her side and forced her to drive his crumpled vehicle.

"There," he said, and came around the front.

He pulled the mouthpiece out. All hopes for making it out of this situation alive vanished. If he was going to let her hear his real voice, he planned to kill her.

Father, please help me.

With a sweeping bow, Echo ripped his mask free and smiled down on her.

"Tim?"

"In the flesh." He bowed again, and when he came up, his eyes were glazed and foreign to the man she'd come to know this week.

"How? Why? I don't understand."

He smiled, then his lips twisted in a derisive smirk. "You soon will, my sweet. You soon will."

Luke slid his card down the reader and jerked the office door open. The building was empty and dark. Taking the stairs two at a time, he charged up to his office. The wall clock said it had taken him thirty-two minutes to arrive. Not that he needed to look at the clock. He'd been staring at his watch for the past half hour. That is, when he wasn't honking his horn and fighting his way through heavy traffic.

The table where Dani's computer usually sat held only a

notepad. Everything else was gone. Of course it was. She'd have taken her computer and all her files to the safe house with her.

"Think." He pounded his head.

Maybe she'd written the address or the man's name on the notepad. He'd seen on television how investigators rubbed a pencil over the pad to see what had been written. It was worth a try. He took the pad to his desk, where he found a pencil in his drawer. He rubbed it across the paper, and the name Anthony Jackson became clear.

Anthony Jackson was Hawk and Tim's stepfather. Was he the owner of Computer Care's building? If so, was it a coincidence or was Tim involved in this somehow?

Maybe Jackson knew where Dani was going after their meeting. Luke grabbed Tim's file and dialed the emergency number listed next to his stepfather's name.

"Jackson," he answered gruffly.

"This is Luke Baldwin. I'm Tim Revello's partner and need some information from you."

"Make it quick, Baldwin. I'm getting on a plane."

"I'm trying to locate an investigator working for me," he said. "Her name's Dani Justice and I think she had a meeting with you."

"She did, but she never showed."

Gut-wrenching, immobilizing worry dropped on Luke like a thousand-pound weight. "She needed to know who rented the Computer Care building."

He snorted. "Just like Tim not to tell you that he had a business on the side."

"So Tim owns Computer Care?"

"Yes."

Shocked, Luke fell back in his chair. Could Tim be a killer, and did he have Dani? If so, Luke had to get to her. "I need your office address."

He barked out his address. "Now, if you don't mind, my pilot's waiting."

Already on his feet, Luke disconnected and quickly got into his car, squealing onto the road. At a stoplight, he punched the address into his phone's GPS.

The phone asked him to turn his GPS on, and his heart sank as he remembered the night Dani had told him to turn it off. A night when she'd been safely in the arms of her family. Now because of him she was in danger. Maybe fighting for her life. He could only hope that she'd taken the same route or he might not make it to her before Tim hurt her or, worse yet, killed her.

God, please, I don't deserve Your help here, but let me get to Dani on time.

Tim knelt in front of Dani and tied her feet to the chair.

"Why are you doing this?" she asked.

"You wouldn't give up. No matter how many times I warned you, you kept digging. If you'd gotten to my stepfather before he left town, I'd never have had time to disappear."

"Anthony Jackson is your stepfather?"

"Surprise." He grinned again. "My mother married him a few years ago, and he wants to be ever so helpful to me."

"But I thought a hacker named Echo was behind all of this."

"Surprise again."

Could Tim really be Echo?

The past few days ran through Dani's mind. She saw nothing to link him to the notorious hacker. "You expect me to believe you're Echo?"

"In the flesh."

She could hardly wrap her mind around the news.

"Prove it."

His eyes filled with pride as he shared intimate details of Grace's murder. Details only her killer could possess.

Unbelievable. She'd been working side by side with the man who'd killed Grace. Her stomach roiled and she had to swallow hard to settle it. "Why are you doing this to Luke?"

"Simple. He killed my brother. Maybe not physically, as in, he pulled the trigger, but he was in charge of their mission. It was his responsibility to make sure communications were secure. He should've died, not Hawk."

"So all the time you worked with Luke you planned to betray him."

"Of course." He laughed, and it floated up into the rafters. "When one of the owners from Security-Watchdog put out feelers in the hacking community, 'Echo'—" he paused and put air quotes around his screen name as if he was a different person "—jumped at the chance. What better than to exact my revenge, to get paid to do so and do it right under Luke's nose?"

"You got paid to do your dirty work."

"I know, right? Icing on the cake. And now I've stashed away enough money to get out of the country." He rubbed his hands together. "But first we need to make sure Luke doesn't wind up with his happily-ever-after."

"You've already tanked his company."

He came to his feet, a hot, angry look taking control of his eyes. "Ah, but I haven't killed the woman he fancies himself in love with, now, have I?"

Luke turned onto the road where Anthony Jackson's office was located. Ahead, he spotted an ambulance and two police cars. An officer stood in the road directing traffic.

Luke craned his neck to get a look at the cars. An SUV the same color as Derrick's had been T-boned by another vehicle that seemed to be missing.

Luke's heart sank as he slowly inched forward with the line of cars ahead of him. "Keep it together, man."

The officer held up his hand and the cars in front of Luke

stopped. He pressed his brakes and studied the scene carefully. He spotted a man sitting on the curb. Derrick?

"Oh, no," he mumbled, and slammed his shifter into Park, then jumped out.

He raced toward the woman he was certain was Kat, sitting on the bumper of the ambulance. A man Luke thought to be Mitch hovered over her.

The officer stepped in his path and Luke shoved him off.

"That's gonna cost you a night in jail," the officer said.

"Let him be," Mitch called out. "He's one of us."

The officer let him go and Luke charged over to Kat. "Where's Dani?"

Kat shook her head and tears flowed down her cheeks.

"Derrick saw a man with a black mask take Dani at gunpoint," Mitch said. "Medium build, about five foot eleven, wearing a ski mask. We have a possible address but can't be sure it's correct."

"Explain."

"Dani got a text from Tim telling her the network was hacked," Kat said, looking dazed. "We think Echo lured us out here so he could stop us from getting to the man we were going to see."

"Tim is Echo," Luke said.

"What?" Kat exclaimed.

"Long story I don't have time for now. Has anyone gone after Dani?"

"I just got here," Mitch grumbled. "And I needed to check on my wife first."

"Derrick wanted to go, but the medics needed to tend to his wound," Kat said. "Ethan's staying with Natalie, and Cole's on his way."

"Where's the address Tim was sending you to?"

"I don't remember it exactly, but Dani put it in the car's GPS."

Luke didn't wait for anything else but flew to Derrick's car.

He punched the GPS button and the address popped up on the screen. He entered it into his phone and retraced his steps.

"I'll get a unit on the way to the address," Mitch called out. "And I'll call Cole to give him the address."

Luke wanted to yell out too little too late, but if Dani had been trapped and injured in a car, he'd have taken a moment to make sure she was all right, too. He couldn't fault Mitch for loving his wife.

Luke climbed back into his car and swung around the officer directing traffic.

"Hey," he yelled.

Once clear, Luke floored it. If they chased after him, all the better. He'd have help in freeing Dani.

"Be right back, sweet thing." Tim picked up a torch from the corner of the room and lit it, then exited.

Fear inched up Dani's back, but she fought it down as she struggled against her restraints. The ropes held tight around her chest and legs. Her only hope was to free her hands. She dug at the hard knots but couldn't move them even a fraction of an inch.

She searched the space for anything to help and spotted a rusty shelf bracket dangling from the wall. The end had been snapped off, leaving a sharp edge. She thrust her weight forward, moving the chair an inch. Good. She could move across the room and grab the bracket, then slice through her ropes.

She thrust again. Moved an inch or less. She dug deep for strength and kept jerking her body ahead until she was just a few feet from the wall. Her muscles screamed from exertion, but she heard Tim's footsteps coming back and knew she had to keep moving or she wouldn't have another chance.

She took a deep breath and lurched hard. Her chair wobbled and she fought to keep it upright.

She teetered for a few seconds, then lost her balance and

her chair plummeted to the floor. She jerked her head up so it wouldn't hit.

She heard Tim whistling as his footsteps came thumping closer.

Lord, please, no. Don't let this be the end.

The doorway darkened and Tim filled it. He still held the torch, though it was only smoldering now. "I was going to spare you seeing the flames, but you couldn't sit still like I asked, could you?" He looked around the room. "I guess there are enough things in here to get a good fire burning."

Smoke drifted into the small space. He'd already set fire to the outer room. "Why set the place on fire? Why not just shoot me?"

"If you have to ask me that, you don't know Luke as well as I thought you did."

Recognition dawned. Losing another person he loved, especially in a fire, was the thing Luke feared the most.

Tim crossed the room and started shredding cardboard boxes. He stacked the pieces on the floor. Next, he took papers from an old filing cabinet and added them to the cardboard.

Fear she'd kept in check closed her throat, and she swallowed hard. Thick smoke drifted into the room, stinging her eyes. She closed them and prayed as she'd never prayed before.

EIGHTEEN

On the correct street, Luke thanked God that this area of town saw little traffic, allowing him to get to Dani on time. But his prayer died on his lips as he spotted dark, acrid smoke billowing in the air ahead. Had Tim set fire to one of these warehouses?

God, no. Please, no. I can't lose Dani to a fire.

What was he saying? He couldn't lose her at all. Not now. Not ever.

He floored the gas, racing down the street of abandoned warehouses as he looked for the right address. There at the end of street. A two-story building. Broken windows peppered the second floor, smoke funneling out.

He slammed on his brakes, the rear of his car fishtailing and smashing into the curb. He leaped from the car and ran. Fast and hard. His footfalls echoed through the deserted space. He reached the entrance and stopped to slow his breathing and calm his nerves.

A SEAL didn't rush into any situation unprepared. Especially not one that held enormous consequences.

Standing for a moment while Dani was inside under Tim's control was the hardest thing he'd ever done. He'd rappelled from a chopper, dived in deep seas and jumped from an airplane. None of those struck the same fear in his heart as the thought of losing Dani.

He took one final deep breath, then pressed his arm against his mouth to keep the smoke from his lungs. He drew his weapon and slipped inside. Hazy smoke hung high in the air, swirling, floating like a living, breathing thing. The upper floor venting sucked it high, giving him a good view of the cavernous space. Unfortunately the venting would also accelerate the fire.

Flames licked over wooden rafters dangling from the second floor. It wouldn't be long before they gave way, bringing down the second story. Dead ahead he spotted three doors, all closed. Dani must be behind one of them. He had to move quickly.

He took a step, but the first door opened and a man backed out. Luke darted behind an old filing cabinet and the pain of betrayal cut though his heart when he spotted Tim.

"I'm sorry, Dani," he said. "Really, I am, but Luke's responsible for my brother's death and he deserves to know my pain. Since I couldn't get to his sister in the safe house, losing you in a fire is the best way to show him right now."

Tim blamed him? Luke hadn't had a clue. He'd thought they were cool. Obviously not.

Tim jerked the door closed, but not before Luke heard Dani's strangled cry. Luke's worst fear was coming true. Rage barreled into his chest, and he charged around the cabinet.

Tim flicked a lighter and set a torch burning. He jabbed it at a stack of old paper.

"Stop now or I'll shoot," Luke commanded as he held the gun on Tim.

Tim spun and grinned wide. "No, you won't. You have too much honor to kill in cold blood."

"This wouldn't be killing. It would be justified to save Dani's life."

Tim lowered the torch and ignited the papers. Fire crackled to life, racing greedily up the pages toward the door.

Luke stepped forward. "Put the torch out and get down on the floor."

Tim's eyes went wild, crazed. "No way. It's time for you to pay."

Luke couldn't shoot Tim point-blank, but he had to stop him. Tim came forward, jabbing the torch at Luke. He side-stepped Tim and caught sight of a rotting timber hanging overhead. He raised his gun and fired. The wood cracked.

Tim looked up. The timber snapped and swung precariously as Tim tried to run. Plummeting toward the floor, it caught Tim's shoulder. He went down. The torch shot free.

Luke ran for the torch and stomped it out.

Tim groaned. Luke had a choice—haul Tim outside or save Dani. No choice, really—Dani came first.

Footfalls pounded behind Luke. He spun.

Cole bounded into the room and Luke tossed up a prayer of thanksgiving that the safe house was located nearby.

"Dani," he screamed. "Where is she?"

"Inside. Call an ambulance and free Tim. I'll get her."

Luke didn't wait for agreement but broke through the door. Without venting, the room had filled with thick black smoke. He could barely see Dani sitting in a chair on the far side of the space. Flames danced all around her.

"Dani," he screamed, but she didn't respond.

Arm over his mouth, he picked his way through the room, trying to draw in air through the thick, caustic smoke.

She sat without moving, her head hanging forward. He lifted her face. Her eyes were closed. He felt for a pulse. She had one.

"Hang in there, sweetheart," he said, and reached for the ropes. Smoke burned his eyes and throat, sending him into a coughing spasm.

His fingers fumbled at the knots, and he knew he'd succumb to the smoke long before he freed her. So he scooped her up, chair and all, and ran for the door. His heart thundered in his chest even as he heaved for breath.

His vision faded. The room spun. He wasn't going to make it out.

This must be how his mother and sister had felt in their last moments. Pain speared his heart as strength left his body, and he sank to his knees.

No, Father, no! Let me save her, please. I don't care what happens to me, but she has to live.

With a roar, he pushed to his feet and stumbled toward the door. Cole charged inside and lifted Dani from his arms. Luke heard the wail of an ambulance. Dani would be okay. All strength left his body and the floor rose up to meet him. He took one last look at Cole's back and let the darkness take him.

Light pulled Dani to the surface, but her eyes were too heavy to open. Her throat felt as if she'd swallowed glass. She heard a beep, beep, beep, and something covered her mouth and nose.

Where was she?

She reached up to pull the offending thing free, and a warm hand settled over hers.

"It's oxygen." Luke's voice wrapped around her and gave her peace. "You took in too much smoke, and you need to clear it from your system."

She willed her eyes to open. Luke leaned over her. His face was covered with soot, and a long gash ran down the side of his marvelous face. He'd obviously braved the fire to rescue her, but what about her siblings?

She removed the mask. "Derrick and Kat? Are they okay?"

"Kat broke her arm and has a concussion. She'll need to stay here overnight. Derrick's had a nasty gash to his leg, but otherwise they're fine."

She sighed. "I'm so thankful they weren't seriously hurt."

"Kat already has people signing her cast, and Derrick's been a real trouper."

"And you?" she asked, and held her breath.

"Now that you're awake, I'm great." His lips tipped in his sweet smile and she could hardly breathe.

"You came to save me," she whispered, suddenly feeling very shy. "I knew you would come."

"Did you, now?" he said, smiling.

She grinned. "You're a SEAL and they never leave a man behind."

"Or woman, as the case may be." He ran his gaze over her.

Her heart pounded in her chest. "In all seriousness, thank you for coming to my rescue."

"No thanks needed." He opened his mouth as if to say something more, then closed it.

"Go ahead and say whatever it is you wanted to say."

"It's nothing."

"I almost died, and I really don't want to beat around the bush anymore."

"Okay. I was going to say that I'd be there for you whenever you need if you'll let me."

"I'll more than let you," she said, cupping the side of his cheek. "I *want* you to be there."

"You need to know that I'm still going to get demanding at times." His voice was all raspy from smoke.

"And I'm still stubborn."

"Should be an interesting courtship."

"Ooh." She let a finger trail down his face. "We're courting, are we?"

"I'm in this for the long haul, and I'm hoping you are, too."

"Oh, yeah."

"I love you," he said, his eyes suddenly serious. "More than I thought possible."

"I love you, too," she answered, but barely got the words out before he claimed her lips for a long kiss.

When he pulled back, he grinned. "I guess God's timing was perfect after all."

She laughed. "I could've done without the kidnapping and nearly dying in a fire, but yes, bringing us together at any time is perfect."

"Amen to that." He leaned down and settled his lips on hers again. She twined her arms around his neck and pulled him closer, returning the kiss and savoring the thought that she'd let go of every misgiving and had a future with him.

A male cleared his throat behind them, and Dani was pretty sure it was Derrick. She'd never realized what bad timing her twin had. She expected Luke to pull away, but he lingered a bit longer, teasing her lips with his before drawing back.

Derrick's brow rose. "I see you're both doing okay."

Dani smiled at her brother. "More than okay."

Luke held out his hand for a shake. "Hey, thanks, man. I owe you one."

"What for?" Dani asked.

"I had a little trouble at the warehouse."

"He's being modest." Derrick clapped Luke on the back. "He tried to carry you out, but he succumbed to the smoke near the door. He moved you far enough for Cole to take over, then he keeled over."

"And you pulled me out." Luke clasped Derrick's hand.

"Amazing I could drag such dead weight so far." Derrick grinned, and Dani saw her brother had fully come to accept Luke.

"I'm thankful you ignored the EMTs. If you'd let them bring you to the hospital, I might not be here shaking your hand."

Dani cast a warning look at her brother. "I'd usually lecture you about ignoring medical advice, but in this case, I'm glad you did. Promise me you won't do it again."

Derrick firmly met her gaze. "Not going to make a promise

I can't keep. If someone in the family needs me, I'm there. No matter what. You'd do the same thing, so don't try to deny it."

"He's right," Luke said. "I feel the same way about Natalie…and you." A blush crept up his face.

Dani could hardly believe displaying his feelings for her in front of Derrick could make this rugged SEAL blush.

He glanced away and said quickly, "Let's hope someone like Tim doesn't come into our lives again."

"What happened to Tim?" Dani asked, actually feeling sorry for the guy.

Derrick socked Luke in the shoulder. "Your hero here shot a beam from the ceiling and it pinned Tim to the floor. Cole got him out and he's going to be okay."

The glazed look on Tim's face as he'd lit the fire around her flashed into Dani's mind and made her shudder.

"Hey," Luke said, taking her hand. "He has a police guard 24/7."

"Did he confess to being Echo and taking money from Security-Watchdog to sabotage the software?"

Luke nodded. "And he said he did it because he blamed me for Hawk's death." Luke shook his head. "How could an honorable guy like Hawk have such a troubled brother?"

"I think he's mentally ill."

"If so, he never showed a hint of it. He was always so easygoing and laid-back."

"Hopefully he'll get the help he needs now."

"I'd like to say I hope so, too, but I also want him to pay for what he did to you." Luke ran the backs of his fingers over her cheek and locked gazes with her. Her heartbeat sped up and she was certain he had to be able to hear it thumping.

She forced her eyes from his.

Derrick smirked. "Looks like the two of you are a thing now."

"We were getting to that before we were so rudely interrupted," Luke said, a grin still on his face.

"Well, don't let me keep you apart. I'm off to sign Kat's cast. She's being a real baby about this." He chuckled good-naturedly as he ruffled Dani's hair. "See you later, sis."

She grabbed his hand. "I love you."

"Love you, too," he said, and departed.

Luke lifted Dani into his arms. "Now, where were we?"

"I'm pretty sure you were going to thoroughly kiss me." She met his gaze and heat flared between them.

"That's right. How could I have forgotten something so important?" He settled his lips on hers. She took a clue from him and forgot everything else around them.

EPILOGUE

Luke charged into Dani's living room to answer his phone. He grabbed it from the table and a flash of surprise hit him when he saw the caller ID. He hadn't heard a word from General Wilder in a few months.

"What can I do for you, General?" he answered quickly.

"With the arrest of the Security-Watchdog owners and this whole mess ironed out, we seem to find ourselves without satellite security software."

Luke tried to concentrate on the general's words, but he couldn't take his eyes and mind off Dani as she joined him in the room. She wore a knee-length red dress, and he could only think about how if the phone hadn't rung he would be going down on one knee, ready to propose.

"You have every right to be angry with us," Wilder continued. "But we hope you can understand our position and put all of this in the past."

"I'm not angry, General, and I'd be happy to talk with you about SatCom, but right now I have something very important to do. Can I get back to you on Monday?"

"Monday will be fine."

As Luke disconnected, he smiled at the uncertainty in Wilder's tone. It would do the committee good to wait on him for once.

"Was that General Wilder?" Dani asked.

He nodded. "He wanted to talk to me about buying our software."

"And you blew him off? But that project you landed is barely keeping SatCom running. How can you wait?"

"It's just two days, and there's nothing the committee will do on the weekend anyway." He took her hand and gazed into her eyes. "Besides, I have something far more important to do."

"What could be more important than keeping your company afloat?"

"You," he said as he knelt down. He pulled a small ring box from his pocket and popped the top open.

"Oh." She clutched her hands to her chest and stared wide-eyed.

He chuckled. "I have fallen even more madly and hopelessly in love with you the past few months, and though I have no money for a real ring, I promise to love and cherish you for life. And replace this with a real ring when I can afford it." He took out a Wonder Twins ring that she knew had to have come from Derrick, and held it out. "Will you marry me, Danielle Justice?"

She giggled with happiness. Not only for the proposal but also for Derrick's obvious blessing. "As long as you promise never to call me Danielle again, the answer is absolutely yes."

He slipped the ring on her finger and stood to kiss her.

"I love you more than words can express."

Before he could pull her close, she threw her arms around his neck and planted her lips on his. After a protracted kiss, she leaned back.

"You know," he said, "I'm going to like being married to a woman who doesn't take a backseat."

The doorbell rang and she groaned. "We're already late for Ethan's party, so don't answer."

"It's Natalie."

"Nat?"

"I invited her over to either congratulate me or console me, depending on your answer."

"Did you really think I'd say no?"

He snaked an arm around her waist and dragged her close. "Not if I had anything to say about it."

He lifted her into his arms and hurried to open the door.

Natalie's eyes lit up. "I guess this means you said yes."

Dani nodded. "Put me down, Luke, so I can hug my soon-to-be sister."

He lifted his free hand in an abbreviated salute. "Yes, ma'am."

"You already have him saluting you," Natalie said. "Way to go, Dani."

"Don't let the guy fool you. He's a real pushover."

"Only for you," Natalie said. "Only for you."

At Ethan's house, Dani twirled the Wonder Twins ring on her finger and smiled at Luke as he talked with Derrick. She hadn't expected a proposal, and when Luke got down on one knee, happiness had stolen the breath from her lungs. Now she could hardly stand to be on the other side of the room from him. Their eyes met and she telegraphed her feelings. He excused himself and crossed over to her.

"You look like the cat that ate the canary," he whispered.

"Um, I feel like a contented cat. I think I might purr."

He laughed and pulled her close. "So when do you want to tell your family about our engagement?"

She swiveled to look up at him. "After dinner?"

"Why wait?"

"I want to see if any of my trained siblings notice the ring or my smitten look."

He trailed his finger along her jaw, sending her nerve endings firing. "Not a one of them can possibly miss the smitten look."

She smiled up at him. "I'm guessing it's much like yours."

He clutched her hands between his. "Let's tell them now. I can't wait until after dinner."

"Okay." She grinned. "I'll just gather everyone together."

Before she could move, Ethan came into the room and clapped his hands. "Can everyone come in here, please? I have an announcement to make."

Dani looked up at Luke. "He doesn't know, does he?"

"No. Your siblings may be good investigators, but there's no way he knows. I told no one but Natalie and Derrick and swore them to secrecy."

"I wouldn't put it past Derrick to tell."

Luke laughed. "C'mon. You know we've buried the hatchet and are good buds now."

"Yeah, until he realizes I said yes and you're taking me away from him permanently."

Luke circled an arm around her shoulder. "He knows I support the whole Wonder Twins power thing and acknowledge that you two have a special bond."

Ethan kept needling everyone to join them in the family room, and Dani turned her attention to the family. Jennie slipped under Ethan's arm, and he smiled down on her. The radiance of his smile made Dani hopeful that her relationship with Luke would be as satisfying.

Mitch guided Kat into the room, his hand on her lower back as it often was. Though Kat loved being in control, she'd become a pushover when it came to Mitch. They stopped next to Derrick, who watched Ethan with interest. Cole slipped quietly into the room holding his stepdaughter, Brianna, in his arms. She laid her head on his shoulder, the blond curl looking soft against his rough five-o'clock shadow. Alyssa stood next to him, her hands planted on her son Riley's shoulders. Sitting in the corner, Mitch's sister, Angie, chatted with Natalie.

A warm feeling of contentment slid over Dani, and she snuggled even closer to Luke. She couldn't wait until the were married and he and Natalie were an official part of the Justice family.

Ethan cleared his throat. "It's with great pleasure that I announce Jennie and I are expecting our first child this summer."

A wave of surprise and happiness floated over the room. Alyssa started clapping and everyone joined in. Her siblings rushed over to Ethan and either hugged him or pumped his hand in congratulations.

Jubilant for her brother and Jennie, Dani looked up at Luke. "I think it's a good idea to keep our announcement for another day. I wouldn't want to spoil this moment for them."

Luke smiled down on her. "Timing, my dearest Dani. It's all about God's timing, and I know He would want us to wait to share. But I'm also certain He doesn't want us to push back the wedding day."

She grinned from ear to ear. "Definitely not. We'll be married before you know it."

Luke swept her into his arms, and as his head lowered, she knew their relationship would fulfill them both in ways neither of them could have imagined.

* * * * *

Dear Reader,

Thank you for reading Dani and Luke's story. I really enjoyed writing the fourth story in the Justice Agency series, as I'm a lot like Luke in that I like to plan things in life and—yes, I'll admit it—control things.

I'd like to say I trust in God's timing in my life, but I wonder how often I miss His best by seeing things only from my perspective and not considering the bigger picture. This is true, even though I have seen over and over again in my life that things I wanted to have happen at a certain time were far better in God's timing than in mine.

I hope you've enjoyed all the books in this series. I love to hear from readers. You can reach me through my website, www.susansleeman.com, or in care of Love Inspired Books at 233 Broadway, Suite 1001, New York, NY 10279.

Susan Sleeman

Questions for Discussion

1. Luke loves to control his world. Do you try to control your life, and if so, in what areas?

2. Has trying to control your life helped or hurt? After reading the book, do you think there are ways you can ease up?

3. Dani believed she trusted in God's timing in her life, but it turns out she didn't. Why do you think it took her so long to realize this?

4. Dani feels an overwhelming need to prove herself to her family, even if it means putting herself in danger. Are there areas in your life where you've felt the same need? What did you do?

5. Luke has lost people he cared about and is terrified of loving again. Have you ever felt this way after a relationship ended? If so, how did you work through it?

6. Luke's father was a controlling man and Luke, though he disliked this about his father, has the same tendencies. How about you? Is there something one of your parents did that you thought you'd never do?

7. When Dani realizes she isn't fair to Luke by comparing him to Paul, she keeps silent. Have you ever been unfair to someone and not rectified it? How has that made you feel?

8. Luke feels guilty for things that were beyond his control. Do you or have you felt guilty in similar situations?

If so, how have you handled it or could you handle it in the future?

9. Luke brings Dani's family into the picture without consulting her first. Do you think what he did was justified, or should he have talked to her first?

10. When Luke's mother, sister and his friend Hawk died, Luke turned away from God. Have you ever had anything in your life that made you turn away? How did you come back from it?

11. Which character in the story do you relate most to, and why?

12. Is there a particular scene in the book that you can especially relate to?

13. After finishing the fourth book in the Justice Agency series, I have really come to like all the Justices and the way they care for each other. Yet it often causes problems for them. What about your family? Have you had similar problems, and how have you handled them?

REQUEST YOUR FREE BOOKS!

2 FREE RIVETING INSPIRATIONAL NOVELS
PLUS 2 FREE MYSTERY GIFTS

Love Inspired®
SUSPENSE

YES! Please send me 2 FREE Love Inspired® Suspense novels and my 2 FREE mystery gifts (gifts are worth about $10). After receiving them, if I don't wish to receive any more books, I can return the shipping statement marked "cancel." If I don't cancel, I will receive 4 brand-new novels every month and be billed just $4.74 per book in the U.S. or $5.24 per book in Canada. That's a savings of at least 21% off the cover price. It's quite a bargain! Shipping and handling is just 50¢ per book in the U.S. and 75¢ per book in Canada.* I understand that accepting the 2 free books and gifts places me under no obligation to buy anything. I can always return a shipment and cancel at any time. Even if I never buy another book, the two free books and gifts are mine to keep forever.

123/323 IDN F5AC

Name _____ (PLEASE PRINT)

Address _____ Apt. #

City _____ State/Prov. _____ Zip/Postal Code

Signature (if under 18, a parent or guardian must sign)

Mail to the Harlequin® Reader Service:
IN U.S.A.: P.O. Box 1867, Buffalo, NY 14240-1867
IN CANADA: P.O. Box 609, Fort Erie, Ontario L2A 5X3

**Are you a current subscriber to Love Inspired Suspense books
and want to receive the larger-print edition?
Call 1-800-873-8635 or visit www.ReaderService.com.**

* Terms and prices subject to change without notice. Prices do not include applicable taxes. Sales tax applicable in N.Y. Canadian residents will be charged applicable taxes. Offer not valid in Quebec. This offer is limited to one order per household. Not valid for current subscribers to Love Inspired Suspense books. All orders subject to credit approval. Credit or debit balances in a customer's account(s) may be offset by any other outstanding balance owed by or to the customer. Please allow 4 to 6 weeks for delivery. Offer available while quantities last.

Your Privacy—The Harlequin® Reader Service is committed to protecting your privacy. Our Privacy Policy is available online at www.ReaderService.com or upon request from the Harlequin Reader Service.
We make a portion of our mailing list available to reputable third parties that offer products we believe may interest you. If you prefer that we not exchange your name with third parties, or if you wish to clarify or modify your communication preferences, please visit us at www.ReaderService.com/consumerchoice or write to us at Harlequin Reader Service Preference Service, P.O. Box 9062, Buffalo, NY 14269. Include your complete name and address.

LIS13R

Love Inspired® SUSPENSE

RIVETING INSPIRATIONAL ROMANCE

CHRISTMAS COMES WRAPPED IN DANGER...

HOLIDAY HERO by SHIRLEE McCOY

Emma Fairchild never expected to find trouble in sleepy
Sagebrush, Texas. But when she's attacked and left for dead in her
own diner, her childhood friend turned K-9 cop Lucas Harwood offers
a chance at justice—and love.

RESCUING CHRISTMAS by TERRI REED

She escaped a kidnapper, but now a killer has set his sights on K-9 dog
trainer Lily Anderson. When fellow officer Jarrod Evans appoints himself
her bodyguard, Lily knows more than her life is at risk—so is her heart.

**Texas K-9 Unit: These lawmen solve the toughest
cases with the help of their brave canine partners**

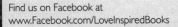

TEXAS K-9 UNIT

TEXAS K-9 UNIT CHRISTMAS
2-in-1 by SHIRLEE McCOY and TERRI REED

*Available November 2013 wherever
Love Inspired Suspense books are sold.*

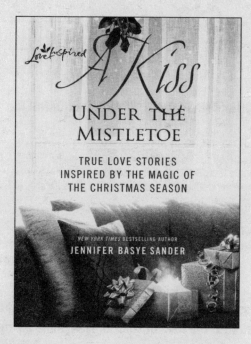

Christmas has a way of reminding us of what really matters—and what could be more important than our loved ones? From husbands and wives to boyfriends and girlfriends to long-lost loves, the real-life romances in this book are surrounded by the joy and blessings of the Christmas season.

Featuring stories by favorite Love Inspired authors, this collection will warm your heart and soothe your soul through the long winter. *A Kiss Under the Mistletoe* beautifully celebrates the way love and faith can transform a cold day in December into the most magical day of the year.

On sale October 29!